Tulika Dubey holds a master's degree in French Language and Literature from Jawaharlal Nehru University, New Delhi. Originally from Bihar, she lives in Munich, where she works as a senior manager in a corporate company. Her writing explores characters grappling with conflicted emotions, a theme that has shaped her storytelling.

In the past, her work has been published by Penguin Random House in the short-story anthology *Something Happened on the Way to Heaven*, edited by Sudha Murthy. She has also contributed as a freelance TV critic for *Times of India Digital*.

In 2016, she self-published her debut novel, *Where's My Story*, a JNU-based campus novel that received widespread appreciation. *When the Past Came Calling* is her second book. When not writing, she enjoys reading and travelling with her six-year-old son, Neil.

WHEN THE PAST CAME CALLING

TULIKA DUBEY

Om Books International

First published in 2026 by

Om Books International

Corporate & Editorial Office
A-12, Sector 64, Noida 201 301
Uttar Pradesh, India
Phone: +91 120 477 4100
Email: editorial@ombooks.com
Website: www.ombooksinternational.com

Sales Office
107, Ansari Road, Darya Ganj,
New Delhi 110 002, India
Phone: +91 11 4000 9000
Email: sales@ombooks.com
Website: www.ombooks.com

ISBN: 978-93-6395-637-7

Printed in India

10 9 8 7 6 5 4 3 2 1

To Neil

My son, my best friend and my life's pillar—
your love and support light the way

One

A sudden call had caused everything around her to pause, except for an unwelcome train of thoughts hurtling unchecked into the dark precipices of her mind—those she had long assumed buried and done away with. It had been twelve years since that fateful night when they had last met. Her life had undergone an ocean of changes since then, but today, repressed memories from the other side of the decade, sprang into the present like phantom pain, waiting to pounce on an erratic rainy night.

Hearing his voice after so many years did not repel her to the degree she had imagined, but an odd, uncomfortable sensation in her stomach made her mildly uneasy. She could not speak much, as he did not wait for an answer … or did he? It was hard to remember how the conversation went. The signals in her brain had momentarily jammed.

Darsh Purohit was going to visit. After years of no contact, he had found her, rung her, and announced this without preamble.

She tossed her mobile to the far side of her bed, trying to distance herself from it. The queasiness was hard to ignore as she attempted to get up. The bedroom walls seemed to close in around her. Knowing what that meant, she sat back down and buried her head between her knees, waiting for the searing pain to come. She had lived with this claustrophobia-inducing panic for a few years, until the sands of time took pity on her and the episodes receded in intensity and frequency.

It's all in the past, she told herself firmly, drawing in long breaths—and just like that, it was over. She looked up and glanced around her room. The walls were fine. The pain had not come. She was fine. Even if Darsh brought the past back into her house tomorrow, she would deal with it like an adult.

The next day began just like any other. She went up to her terrace and felt instantly happy at the riot of colour that welcomed her in the form of her garden. A bunch of red roses had bloomed overnight, contrasting beautifully with the yellow marigolds that dominated the front row. Tall shoots flaunting bright pink chrysanthemums and lilies towered over from behind, as if competing for attention. Combined with the burst of colour, the floral scents never failed to cast a magical effect on her. Her garden was a living, breathing presence—something she had created from nothing. It gave her a feeling of warmth and love that she was incapable of receiving from humans.

Charged after spending the sunrise with her beloved plants, even potting a new one, she followed up with her usual green tea and a warm shower. She went to work, wrapped up two long meetings, locked in a new project, and drove back feeling accomplished and content. Her life was complete. She was a successful leader, heading the analytics department of a reputed company. She rented a beautiful villa in one of Bangalore's most popular locations, drove a sleek red Honda Civic, and made more money than any of her friends back in her hometown. Except for a conspicuously absent love life – which was a frequent bone of contention with her mother – she was perfectly happy: a far cry from the Kavya he knew.

But as dusk arrived and the shadows crept out to chase the fragments of the sinking sun, Kavya perceived her heartbeat quicken just a notch. It was natural, she assured herself. It had been forever, and he had been very important to her once upon a time. *And the cause of all her misery* ... her mind reminded her quietly.

However, when she saw him at her door an hour later, with a sleek carry-on suitcase and a smile, her first thought was to drop the 'adult' act and slam the door in his face.

He looked exactly as he had a decade ago, save for a few fine lines etched around his eyes. His skin glowed annoyingly, and he was in ridiculously good shape, his tall frame filling her entire doorway without apology. Formals replaced the unwashed jeans from college days, and each strand of his erstwhile unruly hair was perfectly in place. The hazel eyes that had always set him apart peered at her the same way, threatening instant emotional upheaval even as his face broke into a warm smile.

So, he had changed. Darsh, whom she had grown up with – the reticent academic prodigy of Parvatnagar – never smiled. And on the rare occasions he did, there was nothing warm about it.

'You want to do what?' she asked him incredulously, a few moments later in her living room.

He had removed his shoes, loosened his tie, and was just short of sprawling on the sofa.

'Three weeks, max. The clerk fucked up. The hotel she booked is three hours away.'

'But you ... you can't stay here!'

'Why? You're not short on space. I'll be invisible, I promise.'

Why? Because the last time you saw me, you destroyed me. Because you don't even remember.

'It would not be OK. What are my neighbours going to think?'

He looked at her blankly, as if giving her time to realise how lame that sounded.

She had planned to deal with this like an adult, but in her mind, she was a teenager again, struggling to refuse him. And while she was mentally chastising herself, he strolled over to the tiny bookshelf above the TV on the central wall. He used to devour books and had read everything under the sun by the time he finished college. Being judged for her reading choices was the last thing she wanted from him. No, not the last thing. Her heart leapt into her mouth when she noticed the book he had just plucked from the shelf. She had bought it five years ago, in a moment of rebellion against her past, to prove to herself that she was indifferent to whatever had happened.

'Ah, *The Stranger*. Did you grow to like it, then? I never got mine back from you, did I?'

The thin thread of self-control almost snapped at this unfortunate reference from the past.

She had to get far away from him before she lost all the poise she was pretending to have.

'Yeah, I don't know what happened to it.' Her words were clear and flat as she got up and reached for her car keys on the table. 'For tonight, you can stay in the downstairs room. I'll return late, but don't make yourself too comfortable.'

She drove aimlessly for some time, toying with the idea of not going back at all.

Bangalore nights were still pleasant, even though the temperature soared comparatively during the day.

The past had come calling. Darsh Purohit – the bad influence, in her mother's words – had just walked in and chased her away from her own house.

The onslaught of memories had just begun. The parts she had buried deep in her subconscious threatened to surface, and she drove faster. It didn't do anything to soothe her nerves. She felt something cold rise in the pit of her stomach again. Her eyes swept the area around her, and she realised she had crossed into the uninhabited part of the neighbourhood. The roads were deserted, and the bushes on the roadside were menacingly dark. Her heartbeat quickened to a dangerous level, and she could feel herself sweating. Knowing what this meant, she made a U-turn, even as it became harder to concentrate.

When she reached the front of the nearest coffee outlet, she killed the engine and rested her head on the steering wheel, focusing on her breathing.

It was not just Darsh who had come back. The panic attacks were resurfacing as well.

Two

In the early nineties, the steel business was just beginning to thrive in Parvatnagar, an idyllic valley-town surrounded by hills and flanked with scenic dams on lakes that roared in the monsoons and gurgled in summers. The residential blocks were meticulously planned—long rows of red brick houses lined with leafy trees that made dense canopies over slumbering streets. Around a recently established steel plant on the outskirts of the town, exclusive colonies were beginning to come up for the factory officials, and tall bellowing furnaces had sprung up with a promise of rapid development in the otherwise sleepy town.

Narayan Purohit's bungalow sprawled across a ten-acre property not far from the steel mill. It was an anomaly compared to the standard houses around the area, but he owned considerable land in Parvatnagar, and selling it to industrialists had put him in a position of power in the newly transitioned machine town. Stories about him filling his coffers indiscriminately with bribes had been doing the rounds for a year. That explained some of the scrutiny Darsh Purohit went through while growing up, but he was also a fascinating subject in his own right.

When most rich kids were preoccupied with branded clothes and accessories, he walked around in a pair of ragged old jeans and a plain grey T-shirt for days, still managing to attract everyone's attention. His mother, who traced her lineage to some erstwhile nobility with roots as far as Afghanistan, had passed on to him perfectly chiselled features along with a tawny beige complexion and hazel eyes that made him stand out wherever he went. Coupled with a naturally athletic build that developed as he crossed into his late teens, his looks alone had turned him into a celebrity by the time he was in high school.

By the time he reached his twelfth year in school, his oddly stark reticence and his dislike for social interactions had reached its zenith. The townsfolk regarded him with contempt because he found adherence to norms unnecessary and did not care to pretend otherwise. But this rebelliousness also made him popular with younger kids who were attracted to his enigmatic person. The sundry complaints from parents to the school board did not affect him in any way, as the board was happy to look the other way owing to his impeccable academic credentials that brought state-wide fame to the small-town school.

A lot of people in town had some idea about his troubled childhood, but no one had seen it first-hand except Kavya. It was the year 1994 when her family had moved into a government-allotted duplex house adjacent to his property. She had been mesmerised by her new neighbour from the moment she had laid eyes on him. He was a quiet eleven-year-old boy, often seen playing on his own around his huge white bungalow, never speaking to anyone. When they became friends due to her persistence, he taught her things that seemed miraculous to her seven-year-old self. To ride a bicycle, to separate egg whites from the yolk, to multiply and divide without a pencil.

Owing to their moving towns in the middle of the academic year, she had to repeat a year at school, making her older than the other students in her class. It was Darsh who tutored her in the evenings and did her homework. In return, she would often lie to his father for him so he could stay out late at night. He hated his home. She knew it because he hardly spoke to his parents and put off going inside the bungalow for as long as he could. Many nights were spent with her, where she just sat out the silent hours with him, like a faithful dog. He was not a communicator even as a child, which suited Kavya just fine for a few years. Things started changing when they turned teenagers.

His parents divorced when he was thirteen. When his mother left, it caused a scandal, and people never hesitated to bring it up when discussing his anti-social behaviour, even after years. From next door, Kavya had watched his life unfold like reflections in a kaleidoscope. His parents would lose all sense of time and space and sometimes even argue in the garden. The noise from their quarrelling filtered through the quiet town and into her house. She could imagine him locked in his room, drowning out the commotion with big headphones.

There were stories of violence with him and around him, and Kavya started noticing bruises on him. When his parents separated, he started disappearing for entire nights. Sometimes, he would take her with him on a motorbike that he was too young to ride. They would ride deep into the hills, through small pathways in the jungle, leaving civilisation behind. He was mostly silent, and the conversations were always impersonal when he talked. Sometimes, Kavya would talk about herself, and he would remain expressionless as if he were already somewhere else in his head, but it never bothered her. These occasional nocturnal riding trips were risks for Kavya, but she always managed to get back before her parents woke up.

In his final year of school, when Kavya was in the eighth standard, he moved out of the bungalow to a spare outhouse on the property. From her window upstairs, she could see the entry of this new shelter. He never got along with his father, but moving away from the main house was a final act of rebellion. She was never asked to visit or explicitly told about it. The few times she had gone to see him there, uninvited, because she hadn't seen him for days, the place had been locked. Leaving notes was not an option, as he never acknowledged them. During his reclusive phases, the sound of a quiet flick of the light switch at odd hours from beyond her window was the only way to know he existed.

One night, in the wee hours after one such hiatus, a soft mud ball crashed on her window. That was his typical way of asking her for a ride. She had not seen him for weeks, and even though slight pangs of anger had started to develop, she sneaked through the back door and climbed the wall.

'Where have you been?' she asked as soon as she saw him.

He started his bike's engine and signalled for her to sit.

'We are going beyond the hills. There's a wild creek you must see.'

'But where were you?'

'Here and there. Let's go.'

She sat behind him obediently. He had come looking for her to have a quiet ride like earlier days, where no conversation was necessary. But Kavya didn't feel like earlier days anymore. She had wondered more than once about the health of this friendship where she had no say in his life. She was fourteen now, and new questions about their equation had started floating through her mind.

The creek was beautiful but eerie at this time of the morning. The dawn was beginning to break, and the air filled with bird sounds. Surrounded by a sparse forest, a line of trees seemed to stare down over the softly running water. The water was clear and made a low sloshing sound as it went over moss-covered rocks. They sat on the bank of the stream and let their toes dip in the cold water. Neither said anything for a while, and the only sound came from leaves falling from low-hanging branches that made rings on the water's surface.

Away from the populace, in the cradle of the raw universe, Kavya stole an uneasy look at Darsh, trying to guess where he had been for those past days. He sat there unaware, staring intently at the spidery roots of the trees across the creek. They spread all over the forest floor, entwined intricately. He wasn't ignoring her; he was studying the trees. She knew that the things most people didn't care about fascinated him, and those they cared about bored him.

'Darsh…'

'Hmm?'

'You didn't come home for two days. I know because the lights in your room were never switched on.'

He kept staring at the roots. A couple of rats had appeared, squeaking at each other.

'You won't tell me?' she pushed.

'The rats, see them? They are fighting hard,' he said without taking his eyes off the rodents going at each other. He picked up a tiny piece of rock and threw it near them, causing them to scurry away. 'A lot of times, people are also like rats. Neither knows when to shut up.'

The implied insult was enough to shut Kavya up. They spent the rest of the time in silence, lying on the grass, staring up at the tinge of blue in the sky and a few stubborn stars that refused to disappear.

'You know there's an interesting play called *No Exit* that I read some time ago,' he said after a long pause. 'It's about some people dying and going to hell.'

She didn't respond, deciding that he was going crazy and this would be her last outing with him.

'Except that hell is just a room with no exit and a few people thrown in together for eternity.'

'That doesn't make any sense. Must be a stupid play,' she said.

'It makes a lot of sense. It means that Hell, actually, is people.'

Three

Narayan Purohit was usually travelling out of town, and even when he was not, he rarely made social calls to middle-class families. Therefore, when he came calling at Kavya's house one morning, she was both wary and curious. Her mother fussed over him like royalty, offering him tea several times and bringing out her finest crockery containing snacks he didn't even touch. He was in a shiny business suit, a Rolex watch dangling ostensibly on his right hand. His hair was combed back, revealing a receding hairline and a creased forehead, but his face had the same captivating quality as his son's. While he spoke, Kavya, however, chose to look at his elaborately printed tie.

'Kavya beta – I don't know if you already know – Darsh's mother is in the last stages of cancer. She wants him to spend some time with her, but he, well, has shown little interest...'

She saw her mother stifle a gasp. She couldn't tell if she was shocked by the news of cancer or Darsh's 'little interest'. Kavya was taken aback by the first one; the second part she had come to expect.

She waited for him to explain what she could do in this situation.

'He talks to you, right? Tell him to go and visit her for some time. He does not listen to me.'

After the initial shock of the cancer news, she let herself revel in the fact that Darsh's dad thought she had some power over him. But that was not true. He had hardly been interested in meeting with her for a long time, and whatever she learnt about him was through school gossip.

There was no dearth of people wanting to break into his world. He was undisputedly the most sought-after guy in her school, and his stories were still part of corridor conversations even after he graduated. The teachers were awed by his brains, the students with his introversion, and the girls because he looked straight out of a modelling magazine, well out of their league. According to the school grapevine, when he found an anonymous love letter in his notebook years ago, it took him five minutes to identify the girl who had written it. He called her out in class in front of everyone and handed it back, announcing that reading it bored him, and it would be wise not to bother him again.

To realise that his father acknowledged that only she could reach him, on some level, made her feel quite important. For some time, she had also been internally battling with conflicted feelings. She was at an age where her friends often talked about guys they liked, but Kavya was left speechless when they made assumptions about her and Darsh. He was certainly not her boyfriend, but growing up in his shadow had left her no space to think of anyone else. However, every time they met, she would return home disappointed by his growing indifference not just to her but to the world in general. She had wanted to cut off at times, hoping it would make her disinterested as well, but whenever a mud ball came crashing on her window, it sent her scurrying down to him. Now, when she was almost seventeen, she was sure she wanted more from him, but there was no way to tell him that.

The request from Darsh's father that day presented her an opportunity to put him through a test. If he did change his mind upon her intervention, it would mean there was something under that rough, unyielding exterior that strummed occasionally, and that she, Kavya Agarwal, was allowed to touch the strings.

While Kavya mulled over the predicament quietly hours after the dad left, her mother was also not over the news.

'What a heartless boy! I don't know why you continue talking to him.'

'He is not so bad if you know him well,' Kavya muttered defensively.

'How well do you know him? I hope you are not meeting him without telling me. I don't trust this boy.'

Kavya ignored that and switched on the TV while her mother muttered her anxieties about the weird boy who didn't care about his mother to the house.

'I don't know why he has no other friends but keeps talking to you. You need to stay away from him…'

I don't know why he has no other friends but keeps talking to you.

Kavya's adolescent heart did some overthinking that night. He was unapproachable to his father but would come looking for her at odd hours. She had been a constant in his life for nearly ten years, and her mother thought he liked her more than a friend. Maybe she needed to confront him directly about where they were going. Maybe their situation was not as hopeless as she thought it to be. The questions kept her awake all night.

At around four in the morning, when she heard the flick of the familiar switch, she got up, pulled on a sweater and a pair of jeans hurriedly, and sneaked out the back door. She landed with a soft thud across the boundary wall, which caused Darsh to peek out the door. He sent her a dithering look and hesitated momentarily before opening the door wider for her to come in.

Following him inside, she caught a whiff of alcohol. It was the first time she was inside his makeshift home. The place was bathed in dim yellow light, making it look drab and depressing. The bed was unmade, and the corners of his blanket were touching the floor. She could see a study desk covered with three towers of books and a lamp hanging loosely from the socket over the table. An ashtray was tossed on the floor. While he was in the bathroom, she sat gingerly on the edge of his bed, wondering if it was a good idea at all to have come. He came back out looking displeased, wiping his face with a towel, his eyes dark and his hair tousled with water. The bravado Kavya felt until now escaped from the broken window pane across the room.

'Why are you here at this time?' he asked curtly, not attempting to hide his displeasure.

'Well, if you can decide to see me anytime you like, so can I,' she answered defiantly.

He tossed the towel aside and plopped himself on the only chair in the room. He then proceeded to put a cigarette in his mouth and light it up.

'Not in the mood for company. I am drunk,' he said after a drag.

There was silence after that. He didn't want a conversation, and she didn't know how to start. The ceiling fan constantly creaked as it spun overhead, making the silence even more uncomfortable. She reached out for a paperweight on his desk in a slightly nervous move. With something to fidget with, she finally spoke.

'Well, umm, this is about your mother. Your father visited me. She is dying, and you should go see her.'

Her announcement was met with a blank gaze, seemingly bored, as if he hadn't heard a word.

'I know you don't feel the need, but sometimes you should do things because others would get some happiness out of it.'

Still no reaction, not a blink. The air in the room was filling up with smoke now, and Kavya coughed, throwing an uncomfortable look at his cigarette. He stubbed it out the next moment and reached for the window behind him to push it open. Kavya continued.

'It's not like you have to fake anything. She's your mother. Visit her for a few days ... and if you...'

'What are you doing there with your hands?' he cut her off as soon as he turned to look back at her.

Disconcerted, she looked down at her sweaty palms that were toying with the paperweight non-stop on their own accord.

He leaned towards her then, taking the paperweight from her clenched hold.

'You seem to be under stress, Kavya,' came the deduction as he carelessly tossed the heavy piece of glass back on the table.

'No, I am not. Anyway…'

'You are,' he interrupted her in a quiet voice and then leaned back on his chair. She saw a tiny smile and a faraway look appear on his face.

'Like years ago, when you barged through my gate, demanding to play with me.'

'Umm…' she tried to interrupt.

'…With fire in her eyes but fear in her heart.'

'Darsh…'

And then he suddenly snapped out of it and got up from his chair, indicating her time was over.

'I am exhausted. You should go. I heard what you said, and the answer is no.'

'But she is dying.'

He opened the door and showed her out. His only reply before he closed the door on her face was so apathetic that she cringed inside, even after knowing him for a decade.

'Everyone dies; it's not as special as people make it out to be.'

Her eyes watered as she walked back to the wall. The news had left her gloomy since morning, but witnessing Darsh's apathy broke her heart. To add insult to injury, he had treated her coldly, almost throwing her out. Everyone was wrong about her being special to him after all. She looked down at her hands in her room, stifling her tears. Her fingers still tingled from his touch, and amidst all the morbid feelings, a pleasant sensation ran through her as she remembered how it felt. This confused state of pleasure and pain, was this what they called love?

Two days later, while going to school, she found herself face to face with Narayan Purohit when his car stopped at the red light alongside her bicycle. She focused all her energy on making the red light green, as she had no desire to face him after her failed mission. He, however, rolled down his window and addressed her clearly, leaving her no option but to look at him with a polite smile.

'Thanks a lot, Kavya,' he said.

As if on cue, the light turned green, and his car swerved past her. She pedalled mechanically as her brain tried processing that acknowledgement. Darsh had agreed to see his mother. A slow smile spread on her face as she felt a tiny reassurance blossoming within her.

Four

The city of Bangalore had seen unprecedented growth in the last few years. Multinationals sprang up all over the city like wild mushrooms. North Bangalore was expanding chaotically, with concrete spreading its tentacles indiscriminately all over the erstwhile garden city. Kavya wondered if she wanted to live here at all. Her office building stood on a busy road, clogged with the ongoing bridge construction and unending traffic. In the one hour it took her to drive from her home's quiet street to her office this morning, she kept thinking about the unwelcome guest at home. That unfeeling loner, who found any conversation longer than fifteen minutes insufferable, had barged into her house uninvited and ignored her refusal to host him. The difficult reticence of his early youth seemed to have been replaced by an easy charm that was entirely unconvincing to her. What was Darsh Purohit up to? She hoped he wouldn't stay long enough for her to find out.

Tired and with her ears ringing from the incessant honking on the road, Kavya punched her card half-heartedly and pushed open the glass door robotically. Her eyes were red from the sleepless night, and she avoided everyone until she got to the privacy of her cabin. Asking her P.A. to cancel all morning appointments, she plunged into the stack of virtual files pending on her drive. She could not bring herself to meet people today; the stress of meeting Darsh had already strung her out.

Around lunchtime, Trisha Mukherjee barged into her room with a half-eaten apple in her hand. Pushing Kavya's laptop away in a clean move, she perched herself on the desk and took a huge bite of the apple.

'Don't yell at your assistant, I charged past her. Something's up, and I can see you don't want to talk about it, but you are telling me anyway,' she declared animatedly, even as her curls sprang loose from her ponytail, covering the sides of her face with unruly ringlets.

'There's nothing up, so let me work. I have a meeting at three.'

'I checked your calendar. You have no meetings today, which is weird. You have cancelled everything. Talk.'

'There's a chair for you to sit in, you know,' Kavya said, waving around at the empty chairs.

'I noticed, but this here gives me a vantage point. Why are your eyes red? Why are you avoiding me? What has happened?'

'I couldn't sleep.'

'Well, I know it was not sex that kept you up since you chase men away with a broom even if they smile at you … so, why couldn't you sleep?'

She wasn't exaggerating. It was common knowledge in the office that Kavya was a workaholic who looked down on romantic liaisons and avoided relationships like the plague. The slightest show of affection made her immensely uncomfortable.

Ignoring Trisha's barb, she tried to wave her away.

'Yes, I don't have your colourful life; no need to rub it in. Let me get back to work.'

'Fine. But we are going out tonight and getting drunk, and you're going to spill the beans!'

Trisha was an unlikely friend. When they first met a couple of years ago, Kavya had judged her for her quirky life choices. She held an obscure position in the content writing department and was perfectly happy with it. She had no ambition and seemed to love getting wasted every other day. She slept with every guy she went out with and was not discreet about it. In an office where a proper dress code was the norm, she wore flamboyant clothes with bangles that jingled every time she moved. If Kavya's mother could see her, it would confirm her theory about her daughter, that she had a thing for 'bad apples'.

She didn't know if she had a thing for bad apples, but people who didn't conform made her feel alive. Choked with layers of proper behaviour and a reserved demeanour that she had imposed on herself, she secretly liked how Trisha lived without a care in the world. Kavya's return to normal life was gradual, and even though she was nearly there, some pieces of her were blatantly missing. Her ability to keep her heart on her sleeve, for example, was permanently lost. It did not help that she had a strong aversion to touch, including platonic gestures of affection. Being with Trisha, to see her living her life uninhibitedly, made her forget her missing pieces.

Although Kavya had hardly shared anything from the past with the woman, her friendship had been crucial. And Trisha perceived her distress the moment she saw her. Only she had access to the woman behind the frigid senior leader.

Going out on weekdays was not really Kavya's thing, but the prospect of getting drunk that night appealed to her. She was in no hurry to go home and look at the face of trouble that had parked itself there.

In a dark, noisy pub on MG Road, three drinks down, when Trisha asked her why she couldn't throw Darsh out of her house if she didn't like him, Kavya replied wearily.

'It's not that simple. We have known each other for a long time.'

'So, what was the deal with the guy? He was your boyfriend?'

Kavya sank into the cushions with a long sigh. She strictly adhered to a two-drink cap on any normal day, especially if she was driving. Today, she needed some more, even after the third one. After all, it was not every day that Darsh Purohit walked into her house with his fake smile and a hidden agenda.

'I could never figure out the deal with the guy, and I think I never will.'

'Well, I am good at puzzles, you know. I should meet this one,' Trisha laughed, inebriated, as she fell back on her cushion, her eyes closing. She was two drinks ahead and about to pass out. Kavya called for the bill just as her phone rang. Her mind, gently swimming in the cocktails she had, registered his name flashing on the screen.

'Hello, Purohit, what do you need now?'

'I am home, and I cannot find your TV remote! Where do you keep it?'

'How does that feel? Not having the control in your hands for once?'

'Huh?'

She giggled into her phone, pleased with herself.

'Yup, Darsh, missing his control for once ... even if it's a remote control ...' She was having a little trouble stressing the correct syllables.

'You seem to be high as fuck. Take a cab, OK?'

'No thanks, I always drive. I don't like being driven. That's giving up control. I like control...'

'I see. And where are you now?'

'Why should I tell you? But then, why should I not? OK, I am in a cute cozy pub. On a road lined with cute cozy pubs. In fact, this road is known for having great pubs one after another. This one has a flashy beer mug at thc cntrance. But I may be somewhere else in ten minutes...' she said and hung up.

She asked for one more drink even though the bill had been paid. Tears pricked her eyes as she remembered their last summer encounter at his bungalow. The eve of her twentieth birthday—a night that was supposed to be the most beautiful in her life. Her fingers trembled slightly as she paid the waiter half an hour later for the extra drink. She was thankful for the amount of alcohol in her system for giving her a sense of control over her feelings. The memories were coming back in stronger waves, but alcohol was good. She could keep the thoughts at bay, those threatening to pull her into the vortex a moment ago. *Good for me,* she silently congratulated herself and looked up to ask the waiter for help with Trisha, but instead saw Darsh's face floating in front of her. *Was she seeing things? Or worse, was he here?*

'Let's go,' he said, offering her his hand. She blinked at him, too surprised to react and then glanced at Trisha, who was now sprawled unconscious at a weird angle.

'She is with you? Can you wake her up enough to walk?'

She shook her head from experience.

'OK. Can you walk?'

She stood up, ignoring his outstretched hand, and nodded haughtily. He then bent down, picked up Trisha's limp body and walked to the lift with natural ease, ignoring the stares. Kavya walked behind him robotically, still surprised that he had turned up. In the basement parking, just when she was about to be placed in the car's back seat, Trisha stirred and opened her eyes.

'Who ... you?' she muttered incoherently.

Darsh ignored her and put her on the backseat, strapping the belt securely. Kavya turned and, from the front seat, gave her hand a gentle, reassuring squeeze.

'Kavya, who is this fuckin' Greek god?'

Knowing Darsh could hear her very clearly, she was instantly embarrassed for her friend, who fell asleep again as the car moved.

He drove quietly as if it was customary to chauffeur two drunk women around at two in the morning. There was no attempt at conversation, and Kavya kept staring at him, conjuring anger from unknown places. Why the façade when she knew he would not feel a thing even if she came under a car? *What was the point of turning everywhere and disturbing her stable life?*

'Why are you doing this?'

'What?'

'Coming here and playing knight?'

'Because life is too precious to play drunk-driving.'

Too drunk to withhold her reaction, she laughed derisively at that response before adding rather caustically, 'Since when do you care about life?'

He ignored her, and she dozed off quickly, waking up when Darsh stopped the car at the address Kavya had given him for Trisha.

'The lane is too tiny for the car to go in. Will you wake her enough so I can walk her to the house?'

Kavya removed her seat belt and turned to shake Trisha by her shoulder, who opened her eyes but still seemed out of it. She climbed out when Kavya explained they had reached her place but stumbled before Darsh caught her hand. She looked up at his face and muttered.

'Oh, you are still here… Is this … going to turn into an erotic dream I am having?'

'Let's get you to your house,' he said, holding her by the elbow as they walked ahead. Kavya watched them but did not feel like getting out of the car. She was drowsy, and even though she hated him, she knew he would safely drop Trisha to her door. She was vaguely aware that he was being unusually nice and did not owe them any of this, but she couldn't care less at that moment.

Five

It was the start of 2006, and Kavya was in the twelfth standard with board exams around the corner. It was a year since Darsh went to see his mother, but her relationship with him remained where it was. She saw him even less now. He had already finished college, and to her, time seemed to be running out. The long breaks made her feel insecure. What were the chances that he was with someone without her knowledge? He hadn't met her for months, and she didn't want to crash his den again at odd hours, especially since her feelings had begun to change.

At school, the classes got intense as the study break was approaching. The teachers had only a month to complete the syllabus, and they were unloading lesson after lesson, like a steady barrage of late shipments at an overcrowded port. The homework turned longer and the deadlines shorter. Kavya was having trouble concentrating on her assignments but did not know how to stop worrying about Darsh.

However, as more weeks went by without any contact from him, she succeeded somewhat in pushing him to the back of her mind in the interest of her impending exams. Her mother had pinned great hopes on her result, considering it to be Kavya's gateway to reputed colleges in Delhi. Personally, Kavya didn't think she was ever going to be at the top of her class like Darsh. She was generally among the top ten students in the class, but her mother insisted she had more potential. That made Kavya feel immensely guilty—that she was squandering her potential because her heart was somewhere else.

During that time, a piece of news reached Kavya that would rob her of sleep for weeks. Biology class had just ended, and they were filing out of the lab when Kavya noticed she had stained her white school shirt with a blob of ink and rushed to the washroom to wash it off. Hiral, who attended biology with her, followed her inside and pulled her aside after checking that all the stalls were empty.

'Purohit is in the news again.'

'Oh yeah?'

'That girl Riya? From the eleventh class? You know, with the skirt two inches higher than needed and full make-up?'

'Yes, the one whose house is full of imported stuff. She can't stop talking about it,' Kavya replied dismissively as she tossed the tissues into the bin.

'Guess who she was having an affair with? All this while.'

Kavya turned to face Hiral with 'are-you-mad' written all over her face.

Riya was a hare-brained, spoilt child whose only appeal rested in the fact that her house was big and her parents were mostly absent, allowing her to throw impromptu parties. Darsh would not have given her one minute of his time.

'Don't believe me, it's your choice. But it's true. She was crying when she called my sister last night. She said she has been calling his home continuously, but he is ignoring all calls.'

'What is she crying about?'

'Your friend dumped her. But not before sleeping with her.'

Kavya laughed at that. An incredulous mocking laugh, also laced with fear.

'Why would she lie about this? I am betting this is true.'

The possibility of this being true sent Kavya's temper flying, and she snapped. 'Even if it is, everyone with sense knows to stay away from him. Who told her to jump in bed with him?'

With that, she started walking away in a huff, but Hiral caught up with her at the exit.

'Talk to him. She sounds quite upset.'

Kavya spent the rest of the day at school in a daze. Her mind felt like a pendulum swinging between rage and fear. This would become a scandal that would shake Parvatnagar. Darsh was long suspected to be trouble by most parents of teenagers because of his unabashed lack of conformity. If the news got out, it could have consequences. He would not care, but she could foresee the damage. Once home, she refused dinner and locked herself in her room on the pretext of studying. There was no other way to keep her mother at bay. She was not yet ready to tell her that her predictions were coming true. Maybe Darsh was nothing but a black sheep.

She drew her curtains aside and looked at the outhouse below. It was locked. Images of him with Riya right under her window flashed in her head, and she mentally recoiled with disgust. She could not shake off a sense of betrayal, but the fear of a scandal weighed stronger. The immediate crisis at hand helped her in bottling down her feelings of personal hurt, at least intermittently.

She heard the door being unlocked around dawn. He was home. Would he care to give her answers if she went? Was she ready to confront him without betraying her feelings? Unable to decide and unable to sleep, Kavya gulped some Benadryl from her bedside table and knocked herself out.

She woke up groggy a few hours later. The sun had climbed up higher on the horizon. She ran her tongue on her unusually parched lips. Her eyelids felt heavier. The thoughts from last night rushed back into her consciousness like wild waves and inundated her mind with dread and anger. There was no use postponing the encounter. She slipped on her chappals and made her way to Darsh's with half-opened eyes but a hyperactive mind.

The door was unlocked, and as she pushed it open, bright sunlight followed her inside, filling the drab room with light. He was sprawled on his stomach, his shirtless back from the waist up on full display. She watched him for a few seconds just because she could. He reminded her of a sculpture on display in a museum, useless if not for its beauty. The light filtered through, falling on part of his face, highlighting the strongly defined features. It wasn't a surprise that girls in Parvatnagar had turned him into a poster boy of sorts.

Reminded of Riya, Kavya came out of her reverie. Angry again, she looked for something to wake him with. A worn-out, small book had fallen on the floor.

She picked it up and glanced at the grim-looking cover, noting the title.

The Stranger by Albert Camus

She threw the book at him. He stirred and then turned, throwing a sleepy, disoriented gaze at her.

'I have some questions,' she stated.

He stared at her with half-opened eyes, not moving an inch.

Under his scrutiny she realised this wasn't probably one of her best calls. What was she doing here? It was inappropriate. He was in bed, and she was standing in his room uninvited. He did not seem very happy at the intrusion. Now unsteady on her feet, she was contemplating walking out hastily when he responded.

'Fire away,' his voice came out groggy as he sat up, his back now against the small headboard of his bed. 'Who doesn't like to wake up and face an inquisition…'

'Riya from 11 B. Did you … umm … sleep with her?' She blurted out the question fast, embarrassed even to say it.

He just squinted at her in response.

'Riya. Round face, short skirt, heavy make-up?' she added.

There was an almost inaudible sigh and then he climbed down from the bed, in a slow, relaxed move as if she hadn't spoken at all, poured two glasses of water and offered one to her.

'Drink. Your eyes look red. Your lips are parched. Your face is tired. Drugged sleep?'

'What?'

'You had something other than water last night?'

His heavy-lidded eyes were not droopy anymore;

they were looking right into hers. The sunlight from the doorway filtered into his eyes, making them glint more than usual, turning from hazel brown to pure glittering gold. They did that quite often, but today, they irked her more, gathering information about the nature of her sleep when she was asking important questions.

'Do not make this about me. I asked you a question.'

'Umm... Riya, you said? I did see a girl last week with that name,' he said as he walked back to his desk to pour himself more water.

'So you don't even know her properly.'

'No, I met her once, but she told me she was studying at that dental college.'

'She goes to our school and hasn't been to classes since you dumped her.'

'Dumped? I met her once.'

'You met the girl once, and you slept with her?'

'Usually, one meeting is enough for that sort of thing. Anyway, why are we talking about this?'

He asked as he sat back in his chair with his tall glass of water. This genuine cluelessness exasperated Kavya.

'Why? She has been telling people at school that she was seeing you, but as soon as you slept with her, you dumped her.'

The only reaction she got was a mildly curious raised eyebrow, followed by two words.

'That's bullshit.'

She kept staring at him while he then proceeded to down all the water.

'Now,' he said as he placed the glass on the table, 'I need a shower, and I am sure your mother is looking for you.'

'Where did you meet her?'

'At the Kailash Club. Like every Saturday, I was watching a documentary.'

'Riya was at a documentary screening?' she asked incredulously.

'Yes, not exactly a school student's favourite place to be.'

With that, he yawned again and got up, losing interest in the subject.

'Go home now.'

'She is quite distraught, Darsh. She has been calling your home, but it seems no one is answering.'

'Oh, that's why the fucking phone has been ringing so often? My ears have been buzzing even out here.'

'So, you plan to answer?'

'No.'

Six

As December approached, the mornings brought a blanket of fog with them that hung heavy over the hills of Parvatnagar, turning familiar everyday sights on the streets into parts of a blurred painting. Kavya sat in a tea stall with a paper cup, steam rising from her hot tea, observing the dark silhouettes of trees across the street, shrouded in a white veil. The early morning chirping of birds and the sound of motors should have been filling up the air by now, but the white monster seemed to have obscured all activity.

Riya Mehta was well known at school because of her rich parents and spoilt manner. She was only in the eleventh standard but carried herself like a grown woman. Hardly ever seen without make-up, she could easily pass for someone older if she wanted to pretend. It annoyed all the other girls that her school skirt was hemmed wider at the bottom, making it shorter than theirs. She insisted it was not on purpose when questioned by teachers, but no one believed that.

Like everyone at school, Kavya had heard stories of her brattish behaviour. Her parents were in an export business that kept them away from home most of the time, leaving Riya alone in her big house filled with imported luxuries from around the world. Like every rich student with absent parents, she had a loyal following, too. They were kids who wanted to spend time at her home, to bask in temporary freedom from their nagging parents. Until now, Kavya had rarely thought about Riya, but she couldn't stop thinking about her since yesterday.

Kailash Club was an elite hangout, and while it was no surprise that Riya had a membership, her running into Darsh during a documentary definitely was. These Saturday movie festivals were not very popular among school students. She knew Darsh was telling the truth; he didn't care enough to lie. The question was, why would Riya come back to his place and then run off to tell a different story?

Hiral arrived on her bicycle, covered in two sweaters and a scarf that allowed only a partial view of her freezing face. She warmed her hands briefly in front of the fire by the stall and took her seat.

'Did you talk to Purohit?' she asked.

'No, not really. He hasn't been around,' Kavya lied.

'Well, she called my sister again, insisting I talk to you. He better take her back, otherwise…'

'Otherwise, what?'

'I don't know, probably blackmail?'

'Doesn't she get it? He does not care; he actually does not. You can't blackmail him.'

'I don't think the parents should know about this, whether he cares or not. They would come for him!'

Kavya felt the threat as loud as a time bomb ticking right into her ear.

'Do you think I should try talking to her?'

Hiral shrugged.

The coaching class next to the stall was beginning to fill up with the twelfth-standard students in the morning batch. Kavya had asked Hiral to meet her a few minutes earlier to find a solution to this crisis. She had not been able to concentrate in any of her classes since the day Hiral first told her about it. Meeting Riya to placate her and ensuring she didn't talk about it to anyone was the only solution she could think of, even though it was a bleak prospect.

'We could go to her house this evening after the physics classes. She lives nearby.'

'Perfect!' Kavya concluded as they joined the class next door. A weak plan was better than no plan.

Riya lived in one of the older neighbourhoods in the centre of the town. Lying to her mother that her evening coaching classes had been extended for a few hours, Kavya followed Hiral's bicycle into narrow streets crowded with pedestrians, even as temperatures dipped after sundown. Cold wind slapped her face vigorously, mentally preparing her to see the girl who slept with Darsh.

The small black gate was already open, and they parked their bicycles on the unkempt lawn in front of her house. The house was huge but, unlike Darsh's, poorly maintained. The unruly ivies were slowly claiming the walls, and the cement was coming away from them in patches, curled and blackened with algae.

Riya received them with a sullen face, as if aware of the fear she had created in Kavya. She didn't wait for a preamble.

'Have you met him, Kavya? I have called him so many times. Someone from his staff picks up and says he is not there ... but I know he is!'

'As far as I know, Darsh—if he doesn't want to, he won't talk to you even if you barge into his house.'

'Whatever happened was his bloody choice. What does he think? He can just wake up and forget about it?'

'It was a foolish thing to do, Riya,' added Hiral, rather timidly. 'Purohit is a weirdo, everyone knows. What were you expecting out of it?'

'I don't need a lecture. He cannot treat me this way. I will ruin him, even if it means telling everyone.'

Kavya made a fresh attempt.

'Riya, listen to me. It's not worth it. I have known him all my life. He has a lot of problems, and he can never be with anyone. It's best to move on.'

'You listen to me! If he continues ignoring me, I will tell my parents he took advantage of me. We will see what happens then.'

She had an intense look that made her threat very real to Kavya. She was vengeful, spoilt unaccustomed to not getting her way.

This was bad news. Both sides were crazy, and she wondered what she was doing in the middle.

When Kavya left a few minutes later, she felt completely out of her depth. A disturbed sixteen-year-old out for revenge. This could not end well. Darsh could be in serious trouble if Riya acted on her threat. The freezing night could not chill her bones as much as that single thought did. Her heart was pounding by the time she reached her neighbourhood and passed Darsh's bungalow, a ghostly white structure against the night sky, looking more ominous than usual. She pedalled on furiously, ignoring it for now, her tyres squeaking loudly against the silence on the road.

A few days passed, and with the danger of failing the boards looming over her, she attempted to plunge herself into her books. But the possibility of a witch-hunt ensuing for Darsh, once Riya told her parents, was real. A police complaint was also possible. If only he could see the implications as clearly as her, things would have been a little simpler.

It was not long before Kavya's mother noticed her frayed nerves. Her pre-board results were out, and she had not done well. She was directly confronted about it at breakfast after her father had left for the mill.

'What's happening behind my back?'

Kavya froze at the question. Had Riya spilled the beans? Did everyone in town know?

'70 per cent? Your father is paying so much for coaching classes for seventy per cent?'

Oh, it was about the boards.

'I will do better in the finals.'

'You have to. Do you want to be stuck here in this small town forever? In a substandard college?'

'No.'

'Tell me what's bothering you?'

'Nothing.'

'I hope you are not in touch with Darsh these days. He is a bad influence.'

'Maa, why do you have to bring him into everything?'

'You stay away from him. There are bad stories doing the rounds about him.'

'Like what?'

'Nothing you should know. But you don't need to hang around with a guy who scores ninety-eight per cent in the board exams and then enrols himself in a local college only to spite his father. Everyone knows he is crazy.'

So the rumour mills were already abuzz. Kavya had never felt so anxious before. What if an angry crowd decided to beat Darsh one night? What if they filed a police complaint? His life would be over in a second. That genius brain of his would take him nowhere. Her thoughts were taking a course of their own. Maybe that's what her mom meant when she said she tended to hyper-react. All day, her mind was conjuring up images of Darsh in jail, and when her telephone rang late in the evening, she got the jolt of her lifetime.

'Tell your friend I will slash away my wrist if he doesn't come to meet me in the next fifteen minutes.'

It was Riya. Frantic. Crying. Crazy.

'What? How? I mean, don't be stupid.'

'Fifteen minutes. At my place. I am alone. And I will do it. I swear.'

She hung up before Kavya could get a word in.

Seven

Every fibre in her body experienced a sudden shock, as if she had touched an exposed wire of a galvanised battery. Collecting herself after a brief spell of immobilising horror, she ran upstairs to check if Darsh's room was unlocked. He wasn't home. Even if he were, he wouldn't have moved an inch. She ran back downstairs to get to her bicycle, grabbed her bicycle and pedalled into the town like her life depended on it.

The main door of the house was unlocked, slightly ajar. Perhaps Riya had kept it open on purpose after her caretaker had left. Kavya went straight to Riya's bedroom at the back of the house, and the scene was dismal. The windows were open even though the night was freezing, and the curtains fluttered noisily. Then her vision, hesitatingly and slowly, fell upon Riya. Lying face down on her bed, with her bleeding hand hanging down the side of the bed, she looked a picture of dejection. Loud sobs incessantly jerked her body, and Kavya slowly registered that the sobs were good. She rushed to her side to check the wound. It wasn't deep, and she hadn't found the nerves. Relieved but still nauseated, she went to find the first-aid box in the adjoining bathroom.

When she urged her gently to let her clean the wound, Riya looked up briefly. Her eyes were swollen from all the crying, and for the first time since it all started, Kavya felt sorry for her.

There was no resistance as she started dabbing the cotton on the wound.

'He didn't come?'

Kavya said nothing.

'He doesn't care even if I die. Let me die.'

Kavya continued to dress the wound almost robotically, afraid of looking up and giving in to the gloom in the room. Riya slipped into an exhausted slumber by the time Kavya finished. After cleaning up in the bathroom, she felt a strong urge to throw up at the situation's futility. Feeling a little dizzy after all the excitement, she walked into the hall and slumped on the sofa.

Flanked by antiques from around the world, the place looked like an exhibition venue. The walls were adorned with pictures, and Kavya spotted a framed picture of Riya's parents smiling from the top of a mountain somewhere. She wondered where they were now and how they would feel if they knew their daughter had just attempted suicide. The right thing to do was to inform them and let the grown-ups take over. But that would mean definite trouble for Darsh. She could not let that happen. What happened tonight had to stay a secret.

She called her mother to ask for her approval to stay the night at Hiral's, saying they would study together to improve her result. Then she went into the kitchen and heated dinner for Riya and herself. It was important to convince Riya that she was on her side.

In a way, Darsh and Riya had some similarities; they had parents who were hardly there, but a house big enough to accommodate a dozen people. Bigger houses made people lonelier, she thought to herself wryly.

Riya wasn't liked much in school for her seemingly shallow and spoilt behaviour. However, today, in her house, heating rice and dal for the injured girl, Kavya was forced to see her in a different light. She was definitely crazy and spoilt, but her suffering was genuine. The garb of revenge had fallen off. Kavya could not brush aside her tearful face from her mind when she had asked hopefully if Darsh had come with her. She saw a longing there, which felt strangely familiar to her because she had been feeling the same for him for years. Even then, she couldn't understand why she felt sympathy for this frustrating brat who had cut her wrist just because she couldn't get him to do what she wanted.

But she was dangerous for Darsh. Kavya had to make this right. When she heard Riya waking up in her bedroom, she picked up the food tray and went to her.

'You know, Riya, I understand how you are feeling.'

'You do? Then will you tell him?' Riya sat up slowly. Her voice came out cracked with exhaustion.

'I will, and I promise you I will get him to meet you once.' Kavya threw this promise in the air like some bargain and saw Riya's eyes light up with renewed hope.

'But that's all. Once. After that, you will move on if he does not change his mind.'

'Yes, whatever, get him to see me once.'

'So, what happened? I mean, what really happened? I need to know everything if I am to help you.'

Riya hesitated, but the promise offered to her made her talk. The story started to unfold exactly as Kavya had expected, but the ending threw her off.

Riya did not meet Darsh at the Kailash Club by chance. She knew he was there every Saturday, so she sat through the 'tortuous' documentary – in her own words – to make his acquaintance. When the movie ended, she tried to chat him up, but he was very laconic and made his way towards the parking. In her bid to be taken seriously, she lied about herself, posing as a college student who was a regular at the screenings.

Darsh, however, asked her straight if she wanted to sleep with him.

'I was shocked, Kavya. And then he started to walk away, and I had to decide in a moment. I did not want him to leave, so I stopped him and said yes.'

Kavya went red in the face, just imagining the scene playing out.

'You didn't find that insulting?'

'No, I don't think he meant it as an insult. It was a straightforward question.'

Kavya believed her. Darsh was totally capable of asking that straightforward question. She knew he would have been mechanically observing Riya and picking up her body language instead of paying attention to what she was saying.

'I said yes to keep him from going.'

'And then?'

'Well, then…' She stopped hesitatingly, as if debating mentally whether to go on.

'Tell me, or I won't be able to help you.'

'You promise you will not tell anyone I told you this? Anyone?'

'I promise,' Kavya said, her heart quickening because she was about to hear the most unpleasant part of the story—the part where she would have to pretend that her heart was not being torn apart.

'I thought he was taking me to his house, but he took me to that ice cream place, got me an ice cream and kind of warmed up to me—at least I felt so…'

'What do you mean warmed up?'

'I mean, he was just nice and smiled too. He is so gorgeous, Kavya!'

'Keep going, please,' Kavya interjected drily.

'He asked me questions about my earrings … he said the design intrigued him or something. I don't even remember. I was so heady.'

Typical. He would talk about stuff that didn't matter.

'So, after that, you went to his place, and you know…'

'Umm … no.'

'No?'

'When we were talking, he asked me where I lived, and I told him. And then back on his bike, I was just so delirious with excitement. You know, this feeling of being so close … like he was mine … I just didn't notice when he turned into my lane…'

'So it was your place where…' Kavya whispered incredulously.

'No, Kavya. He just rode off when I climbed down, realising where we were. Not a word.' She revealed this dejectedly, and her face fell again.

'What?'

'Yes, and I was so surprised I couldn't even ask him when we could meet again. He just rode off.'

'You mean you have been lying all this while about sleeping with him.'

Riya averted her eyes in response.

'I don't believe this—all the drama, this, this!' Kavya said, pointing at her bandaged wrist in bewildered anger.

'You can't go back on your word, Kavya. You can't tell anyone. If you do, I will say you are making it up to save your friend!'

'You are crazy!' Kavya whispered.

'Maybe. I just want him to meet me once. Maybe he thought I was too easy? I am not. I just… want him…'

There was no use reasoning with her, Kavya realised. Her wrist was a sad reminder that she was not thinking straight. Assuring her that she would convince Darsh in a few days – provided she didn't try any more stunts – Kavya left feeling very confused.

So, Darsh did not sleep with her. Why? He had morals? Or was he just astute? And how easily she had assumed that he had! She claimed to be his closest friend, yet she had fallen for the story. All the guilt she felt made her heart go even softer for him. Probably under that bulletproof exterior, he was a gentleman. After discovering this, saving him from Riya's vendetta became even more crucial. Kavya had made that promise to Riya, but how was she going to persuade Darsh to see her? And how long would Riya wait before she started spreading her version far and wide—even to the grown-ups? It occurred to her that Darsh could use his power over Riya to his advantage, but he didn't respond to fear or emotion. This story would have no impact on him.

Eight

The following day, as an answer to her prayers, Kavya ran into Darsh near the city library and decided to accost him. He had a bag filled with books across his shoulder and was just climbing on his motorcycle when she approached him.

'Darsh, I have to tell you something.'

'Tell me,' he replied without even looking up, putting his key into the ignition.

'It's going to take some time. Meet me at Jeeva Lake?'

He looked up and perused her face for a few seconds before dismissing her request. 'Just tell me here.'

'I don't want someone watching us and calling my mother. She thinks you are a bad influence.'

He gave a short laugh at that and started the engine. 'Come sit then, let's go to Jeeva Lake.'

'No, I can't be seen riding with you in daylight … I will meet you there,' she said, even as she felt ashamed of all the sneaking.

He shrugged and rode off. Kavya let out an involuntary sigh, half jealous and half admiring of the complete disregard Darsh had for what people thought about him. He was free in the truest sense of the word.

Jeeva Lake was located at the foot of the eastern hills, around eight kilometres from the city. It had been artificially created some years ago to provide water for the steel plant, but over time, it became the primary drinking water source for the entire city. Even though Kavya had to catch an auto-rickshaw to reach there, she insisted on it as it was a safe spot—crowded in the evenings but deserted in the middle of the day. Even if the conversation was long or heated, they could have the same privacy as his room.

He was there, reading one of the books he had just borrowed, sitting against a boulder under the shade of a big tree. Darsh looked relaxed alone, as if not even waiting for her. Only when she sat beside him did he look up after bookmarking and closing the book.

Kavya did not beat around the bush.

'Have you taken any of her calls? Riya's?'

He said nothing, but a mild exasperation flashed across his face.

'Darsh, try and understand. I met her. She is crazy in her head. Meet her once.'

'I did meet her once. And that's where all this started.'

'She tried slitting her wrist last night because you won't take her calls.'

'What the fuck … and that's supposed to convince me to see her?'

'What's the harm if it gets her out of her misery? It's just once.'

To her chagrin, she saw him start to stand up even before she finished her sentence. He had dismissed the issue and started to walk towards the lake. Something had caught his eye. Once there, he bent down and picked up an object from the shore. When she followed him, angry at his lack of attention towards her, she saw him holding a large black pebble. It was a perfect oval, its edges smoothed by years of being rubbed against the water, almost shining in his hand.

'*How happy is the little Stone / That rambles in the Road Alone…*' he recited, looking content with his find. It was like he had forgotten Kavya's existence in a minute.

'What?' Kavya said, totally bewildered.

'Oh, I was reading this poem by Emily Dickinson just a moment ago when you arrived…' he said, still captivated by the large stone.

The bottled frustration inside Kavya reached a tipping point. Why was she more anxious than him when his future was in danger? How could he be so calm? So fearless?

'You are a stone yourself! Listen to me. She will tell her parents you … raped her, took advantage of her … and they will come after you… The whole town will come after you.'

He didn't even acknowledge her comment. It was as if she hadn't spoken. Exasperated, Kavya shifted her gaze away from him towards the lake. The eerie quietness of the moment suddenly overwhelmed her. She felt tears assailing her eyes, her emotions ready to give in after weeks of bridling.

He looked up when he heard a stifled sob, and that's when she realised she was crying. Pocketing the pebble and reaching for her hand, he joined her in gazing at the placid lake ahead. He laced his fingers with hers in a rare show of warmth and said very slowly, sounding extremely certain, 'Nothing's going to happen to me, Kavya. She is going to get over it in some time.'

After a few minutes of silence, when Kavya composed herself, he egged her towards the bike.

'Sit. I will drop you at the auto-stand when we reach the town.'

The road back to town went through a series of hairpin bends down the hill. Riding through the curves, surrounded by scenic beauty, Kavya's awareness of her physical proximity to him was intensified. She was feeling all kinds of warmth after his hand-holding. Every time the bike made a sharp turn through these steeply inclined bends, she had to tighten her hold on his shoulder, making sure their bodies didn't touch. Trying to keep her mind off the strange desire to wrap her arms around him, she attempted to address the problem again.

'Darsh?'

'Hmm?'

'You should talk to her on a call once, if not meet her. Maybe that's all she wants.'

'No, it sounds like she is obsessing. It will get worse. And I don't respond to blackmail.'

She felt oddly reassured at his plain refusal. The vacuum in her heart left after the cathartic crying began to fill up with desire. She looked around to see if there were any other vehicles on the road. It was deserted. She moved her hand from his shoulder and slowly wrapped it around him. When he did not react, she inched nearer and closed the gap between them. As their bodies touched, she felt a sudden warm rush surge through her. Acting on a strange impulse, she even pressed her breasts harder against his back, wondering if he felt what she was feeling. She became aware of her surroundings only when he stopped.

'We are about to enter the town. You want to push back a little?' He said it in a flat voice without turning around.

She was instantly embarrassed and sat as far back as she could. He dropped her near the auto-stand and rode off. She regretted her loss of control vehemently all through the ride home. Would he have noticed? A part of her wanted him to, and the other squirmed at the thought.

Nine

Trisha woke up groggy but did not feel the full effect of last night's binge drinking until she entered the shower. Water coursed over the knots in her shoulders and down her back but did little to relieve her of the pounding headache. Her body had been doing this for a while now, reminding her that she was not eighteen anymore.

Back in college, almost every night was a party night. She could drink like a fish and attend the morning class the next day like nothing happened. Her friends called her a bottomless alcohol pit, and she thoroughly enjoyed the reputation. Her work life had been slightly different. If her college acquaintances knew she was hanging out with Kavya Agarwal – a prim, no-nonsense virginal woman – for three days a week, they would gasp sharper than the penknife she carried in her purse every day.

But something about Kavya drew her in from the time she met her. It was a boring office party when she spotted her two years ago. A beautiful woman, no doubt, but not even a hair out of place. She looked too meticulous, as if ready to come undone any moment.

She was sitting on an inconspicuous couch at the back of the pub, dressed in a business suit with her hair neatly tied in a tight bun, watching everyone having a good time with an impassive face. Trisha had noticed her toying with her one glass of whisky for over an hour. That woman was only pretending to drink. After a while, she saw two drunk guys plonking themselves on the same couch, not caring that they were about to fall over the lovely, uptight woman sitting in the corner.

She had seen her stiffen the moment they came into the picture, but when one of them crashed into her, her face turned white, and it seemed like her throat closed around a scream. It took some time for other people to disengage the drunk guy from her, who seemed to think he had crashed into his bed. Once she could stand up, she ran towards the restroom like her life depended on it.

Instinct made Trisha follow Kavya to the restroom, where she found her sitting on the floor, her hands hugging her knees, her body jerking with loud sobs. She hesitated but couldn't help herself from reaching out and touching her. Kavya flinched and looked up but couldn't control the tears. Trisha saw her helplessly trying to get a grip on herself, terrified that an obscure employee so low in the ranks had seen her like this.

After a while, when Trisha noticed her calming down, she offered tissues wordlessly and locked the bathroom door. She stood there like a bodyguard, watching Kavya wash her face and apply make-up over her swollen eyes in an attempt to turn back into the cold Ms. K Agarwal, who never let her hair down. They didn't talk that night, but it was the start of a friendship Trisha had never thought herself capable of. Witnessing Kavya in a vulnerable moment had awakened her protective instinct like never before. She had been guarding Kavya's broken soul like a hound for the last two years.

She padded to her bedroom, glancing at the wall clock in the hall. Thirty past ten! She was going to be terribly late again. Not that she cared. Kavya's clout was enough to keep this out of her appraisal, and as for the gossip about her tardiness, she couldn't give a rat's ass.

She was aware of how people looked at her. A self-styled, out-of-control Bengali hippie who slept around and drank too much. For most people here, a woman who slept with her date would qualify as a slut, especially if the dates changed often. She couldn't help if her relationships didn't work out, and she went from one man to another much too fast for the conservative society around her. Just last week, her landlord had warned her about returning too late, and she had almost told him about her running out of fucks to give. It was good she was single when she rented this ground-floor flat. Otherwise, he would have had more things to worry about than her reporting time.

Last night, when she caught a glimpse of the mystery man who dropped them home, it caused a stir in her hibernating heart. This friend from the past that Kavya didn't obviously care about was a bomb. He had looked at her disoriented self with his deep-set honey-coloured eyes and imprinted himself in her vision. Trisha remembered noticing his wiry build, like someone who took his running very seriously. He had even walked her to the house while she clung to him. She definitely needed to find out more about him from Kavya.

Later in the day, she brought him up during her usual visit to Kavya's cabin, asking her to introduce them properly again. However, Kavya, who was generally very supportive of all her romantic liaisons, did not seem too happy about her interest in Darsh.

'Sometimes, you act like you are thirteen, Trisha. He does not live here; I don't even know how long he'll be here. What is this about getting to know him and all?'

'So what? Can't I get to know him for the time he is here?'

'No, forget him. He is not good news.'

'See, I will step aside if you two have a history or something, you know that—'

'Of course not.' Kavya interrupted her sharply but got her tone under control again and added quietly, 'It's just that he is not good boyfriend material.'

'Well, neither am I. All I am asking is for one more meeting. We will see how it goes—'

'Don't be so stupid, Trisha. How long has it been since you broke up with the computer guy? Not even a month ... and here you are...'

'So? Am I supposed to mop the floor with tears for twenty years? Is what you are trying to say? I am trying to move on, OK? And your friend is just the right kind of distraction.'

Kavya didn't know what to say. She did not have a ready reason, but the idea of Trisha around Darsh unsettled her.

'I have never seen you react so strongly about any of my dating prospects. You are right; I think it's out of line for me to—'

Knowing where this was going, Kavya interrupted again, 'It's nothing to do with me, OK? You can strike that thought out. I think you deserve better, but you are right. It's your decision to make.'

'So, you mean we are asking him to dinner?'

'I will try. But I am warning you; he doesn't have much to show under the surface, so don't go raising your hopes.'

Trisha crossed over to her side of the desk at that friendly warning and attempted to hug her, knowing full well she would be stopped.

'You know I don't like that,' Kavya said, putting an arm's length between them.

'Fine, but one day, you are going to hug me back, and I am going to squeeze the life out of you,' Trisha said before leaving with a light spring in her step.

Kavya reached home a little perplexed about this developing situation with Trisha, but decided not to overthink it. She had a new crush every few months. Darsh would be gone soon anyway; he couldn't stay here forever on the vague pretext of delivering lectures. He was hardly at home anyway. Every morning, when Kavya woke up, he would be out running or trekking, rarely back before she left for office. In the evenings, she would already be upstairs in her room when he returned after his meetings. Telling her brain not to worry too much, she had just put her key in the lock when it was opened from inside, leaving her surprised.

'How was your day, Kavya?' Darsh asked her with his usual cheery smile. He still had his work clothes on. Kavya noticed he was wearing her cooking apron over his crisp white shirt, the sleeves folded casually up to his elbows.

'You are back early? Seems like traffic is not so bad after all,' she quipped.

'Exactly the point I am trying to make, that your house is perfect for me to stay.'

As she stepped inside, her eyes fell on the dinner table set for two with an array of dishes, giving the house an aroma of rich cooking.

'Wow, what in the...'

All she could do was look back at him with her mouth open. He laughed as he pulled a chair for her. 'If this could persuade you to let me stay here for the duration of my work, I could do this every day.'

'Oh right, you don't do nice things if you don't need something.'

'Careful, you have hurt my feelings.'

Darsh Purohit was cooking dinner and claiming to have feelings. There was something very wrong.

The dinner was normal, and Kavya could not ignore a rare lift in her mood when they finished. In a reckless moment, she invited Darsh for a post-dinner conversation to her terrace upstairs. Her terrace was her sanctuary because of her precious garden of flowers, and she surprised herself by allowing Darsh, of all people, to see it.

Sitting amid all the colour with the heavily fragrant breeze caressing them, Darsh seemed happily lost in the moment. He asked her a few questions about her plants and showed flattering interest in gardening before leaning back and, closing his eyes, comfortably settled in his rocking chair. The street that her house overlooked was lined with trees that rustled in the night wind, muffling the city noise on the distant roads to a minimum. A

Gulmohar tree formed a protective canopy over the railing, and scarlet flowers carpeted the terrace floor every night. Today was incredibly windy, and as the trees swayed in the strong gusts and dry leaves on the roads wrestled with concrete, she watched him stealthily from the small hanging egg chair she had burrowed herself into.

He had a slight smile, content in the sounds the night was making, unaware of her frank perusal. She felt jealous of how relaxed he looked in her house when she had been on ropes since he arrived.

'What are you thinking about?' she asked to break the silence.

He spoke without opening his eyes, 'Nothing at all. Just breathing in the fragrance … enjoying the breeze.'

'You still don't talk about anything that matters, do you?'

He opened his eyes then and focused his attention on her. 'OK, ask me what you want to know about the things that matter.'

'You don't answer questions either.'

'Try me.'

'What do you do for a living?'

'I am a psychiatrist. And a psychotherapist.'

It caused Kavya to raise her eyebrows.

'Yup, I know, big surprise,' Darsh added.

'Back in the day, you were more a mental patient, Purohit,' she said. It felt good mouthing the words aloud.

'I will have you know that during my MD, all my profs told me this was my only calling.'

'Why?'

'You know what Freud said about psychotherapy? A good therapist is a blank slate. And I was as blank as it gets...'

'Aren't therapists supposed to be warm and friendly?'

'Not necessarily. They need to be objective and attentive, more than anything.'

'But you can't even pretend to be nice.'

'I worked on myself. I am good at my job.'

'And how are you both a therapist and psychiatrist? Is it the same?'

'No, they are not. I started practising as a psychiatrist after my MD and residency. And then I also got a PhD in psychotherapy, leading to a therapist licence.'

'Always the nerd.'

A pause followed, and Kavya found herself dabbling a little into their past life. 'Well, you did cure Riya of her unhealthy obsession with you, so there's that.'

Darsh seemed surprised for a fleeting moment when she brought up something from Parvatnagar so casually, and so was she. Being surrounded by the comfortable aura her plants gave her, she was getting adventurous.

'Weren't you continuously pissed with me till I agreed to meet her?' he let out flippantly, and she smiled, remembering how she had not given up.

'There were so many who got their hearts broken by you back then,' she said it aloud in the same vein of nostalgia, without intending to.

A heavy silence enveloped them after her unwitting remark. She had addressed the elephant in the room, as the biggest heartbreak was her own.

'Kavya…' he began to say something, but she stood up almost abruptly and ended their terrace time right after. She had been yanked back to the past, to that night she had played in her mind repeatedly, like a stuck clip from a horror movie. The sands of time had deposited a steady stream of sediment on those memories, but now, like a ghost from the past, he had turned up and swirled things up again. Her stomach churned with a sudden fear that twisted like a sharp knife in her guts. The calm she had acquired with years of work was going to get snatched away.

Ten

When she woke up the following day, she noticed a piece of paper slipped under her bedroom door. She picked it up and saw that it was an invitation leaflet.

Christ College is happy to invite you to a talk on 'Mental Health & Indian Youth' by Dr Darsh Purohit, MD, (California, USA).

It said 7 p.m., and as Kavya flipped it over, she saw he had scribbled a personal invitation: 'Come hear me out.'

Well, that's rich, she thought wryly, with no intention of going. However, Trisha considered this latest unfolding of events as a heaven-sent opportunity to get together with him. She refused to drop it all day in the office until Kavya agreed grudgingly.

'OK, let's go when it's over. No desire to hear his talk,' she typed hastily to escape her ongoing harassment on the office instant messaging service.

'Even better. That way, we can have a nice long dinner after that, where you can say nice things about me.'

'Bye for now,' she typed with finality and closed the chat window.

Trisha practically herded Kavya out of the office and got her into the car just in time to make it to Darsh's talk. He was already speaking when they entered the auditorium from the backdoor, whispering apologies to people while making their way to the only two empty seats in the last row. The hall was packed. Almost a couple of hundred people were listening to him in rapt attention. Most of them looked young, probably students from around the city, curious about the doctor from the US.

'He doesn't seem as superficial as you said, Kavs,' Trisha whispered without taking her eyes off the stage. Brought out of her reverie, Darsh's words, laced in a mild American accent, started making their way to her ears.

'You need counselling. How often has this phrase been used as a derogation or an insult? It implies you are crazy, not worth my time, or I don't want to do anything with you. Do you see why that approach is inherently wrong?

'It's wrong because it displays our disgust and intolerance for mental suffering.

'A physical ailment such as catching a cold is given more attention than a mental breakdown. Even when it's an unequivocal fact that depression causes way more deaths than seasonal fevers, we refuse to acknowledge it. It's still not real enough to rattle us. It is still something that doesn't exist. But it's claiming more lives than we would like to think.

'How long will mental issues remain ghosts under your bed that haunt you perpetually, unacknowledged by people around you?

'It's essential to learn to notice the signs. Many lives can be saved if we acknowledge that mental health, like physical health, needs to be looked after. To drive my point further home, I would now like to quote some facts and figures.'

The screen behind him changed and displayed a bar graph depicting deaths due to mental illness across the years.

The sinking feeling in the pit of Kavya's stomach was back. Here was a man who did not go to his mother's funeral and was utterly indifferent to an attempted suicide on his account. A man who gave so little of himself to anyone that he remained a stranger in his town. A man who had pushed her into depression unrepentantly. Yet, here he stood, championing mental well-being with a manufactured passion that looked so real, it could even fool her. He claimed to hate imposters, but now, he seemed to be making a living out of being one.

'How many of you have mocked someone when they have expressed feeling anxious or depressed?

'How many of you have friends you can talk to on an off day? That day when you don't want to dress up, don't want to go out, don't want to be cool and fun?

'How many of you have repeatedly called a friend when they don't pick up?'

A sombre silence enveloped the hall as everyone contemplated their behaviour. He was raising questions about their everyday life.

'All you have to do is to listen. No judgements, no solutions. Just being there is enough.'

Kavya felt an onslaught of unwanted memories hurtling towards her without warning. It was a late realisation, but coming to this talk was a careless mistake. The pain she had gone through at the beginning of her descent into hell seemed fresh all over again. And it was the hell that Darsh Purohit engineered for her, pushed her into and never came back to pull her out from.

'Don't be embarrassed talking about professional counselling. If you have taken it, share your experiences openly. Someone might find a way out of their personal hell if they knew about a positive story around them.'

Personal hell. He didn't even know what it meant. He had been indifferent to her suffering even from next door, not once curious about the hell she had to live through back then.

He ended the talk by sharing details on the hospitals he had partnered with and the numbers available for contact. He gave out his email, too, assuring them of complete privacy. Loud applause echoed through the walls as he smiled humbly and left the stage.

Kavya was in a strange dilemma as she got her car out, waiting for Trisha to get Darsh and meet her at the exit. She had sent her to get him to buy some time alone as she had left the auditorium highly perturbed. This man who had walked into her house was an imposter with a hidden intention he refused to reveal. It made Kavya nervous. Did he know? No, that was impossible. It had taken her years to rub off his dark imprint from the fabric of her life. He needed to leave before the chaos in her closet came tumbling out.

She had promised Trisha this impending dinner, but she could not mentally carry banalities in the form of a conversation with him. She needed the safety of her room with a thick physical and metaphorical door between them.

She saw them approaching. Trisha giggled at whatever story he told her, and Kavya felt a cold sweat trickle down her back. How could she let her walk into this, knowing fully what he was capable of? She had to cancel this dinner and thwart all attraction between them.

As soon as they climbed inside, she announced the change of plans, keeping her eyes firmly on the road to avoid facing either of them.

'I am not feeling well, so we must take a rain check on this dinner.'

'Whaaat?' Trisha exclaimed immediately. 'You were OK just a moment ago! What happened all of a sudden?'

She cleared her throat before responding. 'I am exhausted, Trish. I am sorry. I need to get to bed, or I will get too sick for work tomorrow. I can't let that happen.'

Darsh, who was in the rear seat, seemed busy typing on his phone, utterly indifferent to this conversation, so Trisha decided to take the bull by the horns.

'Umm, Darsh, did you hear that? Your friend is getting old. Would you be fine having dinner with me without her? She isn't coming.'

Kavya was slightly angry at Trisha for being insistent, but didn't say anything. She truly wanted to protect her friend, but they were not kids anymore. Trisha had a right to do what she wanted. Also, she did not want Darsh in her house for now.

Darsh looked up from the phone and gave her a quick smile.

'Sure, you must pick the place, though; I don't know the city at all. Kavya, ring me if you need anything, OK?'

'OK, I will drop myself off, and you can take the wheel. I don't need the car until tomorrow,' Kavya added coldly and drove. She couldn't wait to get away from them, to the tranquillity of her bedroom, which promised a good night's sleep because a bottle of antidepressant tablets waited for her in her bedside drawer. Maybe she would do some plant-potting; it always helped her nerves. She waved them a hurried goodbye as she exited the car and made for the door.

Eleven

Once she left, Darsh took the wheel, and they found a small place near Trisha's house to spend the evening. Trisha was a little awkward as Kavya had suddenly removed herself from the plans. Still, Darsh seemed perfectly at ease, giving her his complete attention like he never expected the night to be any different. Trisha studied him carefully all through the dinner. He was meticulous with everything—the order, the cutlery, the mannerisms. It was all too perfect. He asked her questions that showcased his interest in her but avoided being invasive at the same time.

On the other hand, she was sloppy, dropped her fork twice, and tore away at her butter naan with abandon, while every morsel Darsh made before he popped it in his mouth was so neat he did not even need a napkin. Being out with someone so clearly out of her league was intimidating—immensely attractive, highly accomplished, and always in control. She caught herself wishing for two things: that he was single and available, and that he didn't notice her uncouth ways.

In some corner of her mind, though, a little red light blinked because she sensed tension between him and Kavya—something more than a childhood spat. In light of it, it would be inappropriate to want to start anything remotely romantic with him without knowing the whole picture, even when Kavya insisted otherwise. As the dinner ended, she realised she needed more time with him to figure out if she needed to worry about their past.

'Ah, it's difficult getting a cab at this time, peak hour,' she said, looking into her phone as Darsh paid.

'In your city, it's always peak hour. I will drop you, don't worry.'

A while later, when they got into the car, Trisha attempted to take control of the conversation. During dinner, he navigated the chatter and revealed precious little about himself or Kavya.

'So, Darsh, Kavya doesn't talk much about your childhood. You guys were neighbours?'

'Yes, we lived next door to each other.'

'I see … were you guys good friends?'

Darsh paused before replying, keeping his eyes on the road.

'I wasn't good friend material back then … I am now…' He flashed her a sudden ear-to-ear grin, which made her dizzy, and she went off track just a little bit.

'You know you are so damn hot; it's not normal. Were your parents demi-gods or something to give you such genes?'

He kept his eyes on the road and smiled again before answering enigmatically.

'Unfortunately, that's not all they gave me…'

A minute of awkward silence followed before Trisha, although very curious, ignored the loaded comment.

'Anyway, I digress ... so, did you both fight a lot or something? Because frankly, I see no love lost here.'

'No fights, but I am sure she hated me sometimes. Looking back, I think even I would have hated myself.'

'And why are you here now?'

'What is this, an interrogation?' he said to that, but just as Trisha was beginning to apologise, he interrupted.

'I am kidding, Trisha. Well, I am here on an independent project about mental health ... spreading the word, meeting hospital boards, seminars, that sort of thing.'

Trisha knew he wasn't being completely honest but hesitated to point it out.

'But now that I am in Bangalore,' he continued, 'I think it's also something to do with my therapist back in med school who kept insisting I should see Kavya.'

'Oh! Some childhood you both have had! One has panic attacks, and the other one sees a therapist.'

At that point, they had reached her lane, and she signalled for him to park on the side of the main road. They both knew her street was too tiny for the car to pass through. As soon as he parked the car and shut off the engine, he turned to her, curiosity on his face.

'What panic attacks?'

'Well, I don't know much; maybe it's not even a reality anymore. We met some years ago when she was having one. You know what? I feel there's so much more to talk about. Do you wanna come in?'

She added the last part on impulse, hoping it didn't sound like what she thought it sounded like.

Darsh agreed readily and followed her into the lane after confirming that the car was in a safe spot. She quietly instructed him to stay silent while entering the small two-storeyed gated house.

'My landlord lives on the first floor. He thinks I have pretty loose morals, so if he sees you coming in, he will throw me out of the house.'

'Interesting. Having to sneak in like you're eighteen,' he whispered as she opened the iron gate gingerly, hoping to avoid any sound.

Her place was a small BHK, but she had given the living area a distinct personality. She had two large houseplants, one right next to the door and the other beside a large window that overlooked her landlord's garden. Both plants were adorned with string lights that started blinking in different colours when she switched on the lights. The hall led to an open kitchen and was furnished with a noticeable fluffy purple mini sofa, which converted into a bed. Opposite it, across the glass-topped centre table, was a huge recliner, which was Trisha's prize possession. It had cost her a whole month's salary, but she never regretted buying it. It was a living presence for her, giving her comfort, warmth, and love every time she returned after a tiring day.

As Darsh settled on the sofa, she handed him a glass of wine and continued with her story as she settled into her recliner opposite him. She told him how she met Kavya in a bathroom, trying to control her sobs. Although he did not respond outwardly, Trisha could see how the story affected him.

'So, why were you in therapy, and what does it have to do with Kavya?'

'Hmm…' He paused momentarily and then took a large sip from his glass, pondering where to start.

'Well, I was what they call, in medical terms, an emotionally suppressed subject. I learnt this later in my years at the school. But back in Parvatnagar, I thought I was the one who was normal while everyone else was crazy.'

Once he found where to begin, Darsh told her his story effortlessly, like he was talking about someone else. He was more revealing than she had expected. He dissected his past self like a doctor would do with a patient and gave an insight into himself to Trisha that she had hardly imagined possible in a first meeting.

He was a child born out of an incompatible marriage. He had grown up seeing his parents fight often, which had bordered on violence. There were many nights where he had woken up to the sounds of things being thrown in fits of rage downstairs. Adding to that, his father was mostly absent, focused on making money in whichever way possible, and his mother was abusive. She had set impossibly high standards for him, and minor failings irritated her. Due to an ancestry that indicated some nobility, she thought she had married beneath her and hated the ordinary life in Parvatnagar.

The frustration was mainly meted out to Darsh because he could not defend himself. She couldn't tolerate mess and demanded manners at an age when he did not even understand what those were. Being hit and punished frequently in his boyish years turned him indifferent to everybody's pain. His father was never there, too uninterested to interfere in what was going on at home. He felt absolutely nothing for his parents, did not know what familial love was, and never made any friends.

Noticing Darsh had emptied his glass, Trisha sprang up from her recliner and filled it without losing a moment. He was turning more forthright with every passing minute, and it was disarming her. She had anticipated Darsh as a tough, evasive person, but he revealed himself like an open book.

As if aware Trisha had a long night in mind, he removed his shoes and leaned back into her tiny couch, taking another long sip from his glass.

Trisha settled back on her seat close to the kitchen counter where the Grovers bottle she had just opened was in comfortable reach. The door to her cramped bedroom was ajar, and Darsh had a direct view of the unmade bed heaped with clothes. She regretted living in such a mess just a little at that moment. The wind rustled the trees lined outside in the garden, bringing the cool breeze inside in generous spurts, making the night pleasant.

'You look like you are prepared for a story,' Darsh observed, 'curled on your comfy seat, toying with your glass, wrapped up in that blanket, looking at me with expectant eyes…'

'Cheers to your eye for detail…' she replied, smiling. 'And continue…'

'So, a year into med school, somebody suggested I seek therapy because I guess they saw how wrong in the head I was…'

He told her that, at first, he ignored the idea. He used to talk very little and could not address feelings, so therapy didn't seem right. But one of his professors systematically persuaded him into it, telling him that despite being academically brilliant, he was doomed if he didn't get treated.

'My first five sessions were a disaster. There was absolutely no interaction. An hour of silence, and just like that, it was over. But then, one day, I saw my therapist, Candice ... I saw her eyes filling up like she was about to cry ... I opened my mouth to ask her why, but instead, I realised I was the one crying!'

He laughed, recollecting that particular experience.

'Kavya would never believe that,' he added.

'Why was your therapist crying, though?' Trisha asked, curious.

'Maybe she wasn't. Maybe it was my feelings that I was projecting on her. Transference ... but I will never know.'

'Long story short, therapy helped me immensely, and I continued to see Candice for years. My decision to go deeper into mental health and pursue psychiatry resulted from this experience.'

'So, now you want to be Kavya's therapist?' she matter-of-factly asked him. The wine was making her heady now.

'Exactly opposite...'

'Really?'

'I told you ... Candice kept recommending that I meet Kavya as part of my therapy. And now, after so many years, if someone told her I was actually here as Kavya's imposing house guest, she would not believe it at all.'

The second glass was over, too, and then he looked at his watch and realised he had stayed late. Asking if she could book him a driver, he started putting his shoes on.

Trisha didn't want him to go. The tiny crush she had on him when they met for the first time was back, intensified by the great evening they just had. She looked at her phone lazily, thinking of ways to stop him. There was so much to talk about. While he was very forthcoming about himself, he did not reveal much about Kavya.

She still didn't know if he had a romantic history with her, but it seemed to her of little importance now. And Kavya had told her she was free to take things anywhere with him.

'I can't find any driver. That's Bangalore for you … overbooked.' She announced, peering over her phone as if she had tried several times and failed.

'OK, so let's keep trying for a while … there's no way I am going to drive now,' he said and flopped back onto the couch, closing his eyes.

She got up and cleared the table. Her bangles jingled with every movement, fighting the sudden silence in the room. He seemed relaxed. Trisha made a decision then. While walking back from the kitchen, she approached the sofa instead of the recliner and sat beside him, ignoring her inner voice of caution with finality.

It had been so long, and he was so hot, slumped beside her after baring his soul to her.

He opened his eyes when he sensed her beside him and threw her a glance. The blinking string lights danced in his light eyes, making them look hypnotic in an unearthly way. His skin was smooth and shiny, inviting to be touched, and as her eyes rested on his delectable mouth, she tossed all caution to the wind and placed her lips on his. They were warm and tasted of the wine they had shared, but neither welcomed her nor pushed her away.

She decided to go deeper and leaned further to explore his mouth and felt his hand come up on her waist to support her gently as she leaned into him, but there was nothing sexual in his touch. His face was impassive once she finished kissing him and opened her eyes. She could see nothing there. She realised she had made a mistake, but the dominant part of her brain told her it was fine to finish what she started.

'I am very drunk, Darsh.' She heard her rasped voice confessing to him while her eyes stayed fixated on his lips, wanting to kiss again.

He smiled and then stood up from the couch just as she leaned towards him again, causing her to slump down on the now-empty sofa.

'That's why it isn't a good idea.'

'That's not true. It's an excellent idea,' she protested, even as her eyes closed.

Twelve

Riya had called her every day for weeks, hoping Kavya would deliver on her promise. The fact that her board exams were looming didn't help either. She was a nervous wreck, swaying between the fear that Riya might do something irrational any day and the despair of knowing her results would never meet her mother's expectations. School had ended for her batch, and all other twelfth-standard students were burning the midnight oil. But Kavya struggled to focus on physics and chemistry, too entangled in Riya's drama. Instead of revising answers to sample questions on her desk, she was constantly improvising responses to pacify Riya.

The night before her exams began, Kavya broke into a sweat while trying to sleep. She felt an unbearable pressure on her lungs, her body burning despite the ceiling fan spinning at full speed. She walked to her window and opened it, welcoming the slight breeze. The cool air soothed her, as did the dim glow of the light bulb in the room below. He was there—and he was awake.

There was nothing Darsh didn't know from the school curriculum. Until a few years ago, she had spent a lot of time with him revising her syllabus before exams. He would point out what to focus on and help her learn it with ease. But once he left school, his caginess increased—and extended to her as well. The study sessions had simply stopped.

The door to his room opened with a creak, breaking her thoughts. He walked to his bike to collect something. As he returned, he glanced up and caught her looking down at him.

'You look ill,' he said instantly. He didn't need to raise his voice. The town was quiet at this hour, and her window wasn't very high.

'I'm sweating,' she said.

'Boards start tomorrow?'

'Yes.'

'You don't want to be alone.'

'No.'

'Come over.'

His room looked more arranged than usual. The bed was made, so clearly he hadn't been sleeping. The table lamp was on, and *The Stranger* – the same book she had once hit him with – lay open, face down, on the armchair. She had interrupted his reading.

'You can catch up on your sleep here if you want to. I'll wake you up before sunrise—your mother won't know.' He gestured to the bed. She hadn't planned to sleep but climbed up anyway; it looked like the most comfortable option in the room.

He lounged back in his chair, his legs perched on the edge of his desk, a picture of relaxation. The book blocked her view of his face, and she was grateful. It allowed her to stare without hiding the wistful envy she felt. He was always in control—never perturbed, never nervous. How did he manage to live like that, with not a care in the world? A sigh escaped her, and he lowered the book.

'You said something?'

'I'm going to be such a disappointment to Mom. She's already made a list of the top Delhi colleges for me.'

'It's not so bad here. My college is good.'

'It's different for you. You can leave anytime. But this was a way out for me.'

'Way out of what? It's all the same everywhere.'

She let out another frustrated breath, knowing he wouldn't understand. There was no use explaining—he'd lose interest anyway. But to her surprise, he closed the book, placed it on the table, and gave her his full attention. He was going to talk. This was new.

'You don't even know why you want to go to Delhi, do you?'

Kavya shrugged. 'Everyone wants to.'

'So, you want what everyone wants?'

'I don't know what I want. All I know is that my parents really want me to do well in life.'

'You keep wanting to do things for others, don't you?'

'Yes. Is that a bad thing?'

'I wouldn't know. Does it feel good?'

'Sometimes. Like when I told Riya I'd get you to see her once,' she added slyly.

'And you forgot to prepare for your exams in all that excitement?' he continued, expressionless.

'Yes ... you could say that...'

'So to make someone happy – even fake happy – you let go of your own shot at happiness?'

'Umm, no … not like that…'

'So, Riya's happy with your fake promise, but your mother's going to be disappointed. Sounds exactly like that.'

'You're unbelievable!'

'Why not try to figure out what you want?'

With that, he leaned back and picked up the book, signalling that the conversation was over. Darsh's words, though far removed from her reality, seemed tempting. Sometimes their effect was like a drug—inducing a temporary feeling of lightness, daring her to ignore the world as he did. But the moment he was gone, the aura would evaporate. Alone, she was a nervous wreck – always had been – and the whole town knew it. But right now, terrified of staring at a test paper she hadn't prepared for, she wanted to keep the conversation going, to pretend she had things under control.

'I'm sure I won't score below seventy per cent—and that's fine with me.'

'It's fine for you. It's fine for the world…' he replied.

'You're right. Who cares, as long as I don't fail, right?'

'Well, big deal even if you do,' he said, flipping a page.

'Easy for you to say. Do you even know what second position feels like?'

'No, but I have a feeling I wouldn't mind.'

She smirked at that—and saw him turn to look at her.

'It was funny… the 'I have a feeling' part.'

With a tiny shrug, he went back to reading. Kavya looked at the black clock mounted high on the wall, ticking away stealthily. It was going to be three in the morning. She needed to go back to her room, but he was slightly more forthcoming than usual tonight. Perhaps she could make some headway for Riya.

'You know you don't have feelings, right?'

He didn't react.

'Riya calls me every single day. All she wants is to see you once.'

All he did was turn another page, as if she hadn't spoken. He had gone back into his shell, and she felt angry at his unrelenting stance. She climbed down from his bed and wore her slip-on sandals very noisily.

'I don't like it, Darsh. It wasn't a fake promise to me when I made it.'

He still didn't look her way.

'Good night then.'

There was no reaction, even as she stomped off and shut the door behind her.

Her first paper was Chemistry, and it was also a subject she had scored significantly lower in during her pre-boards. Predictably, the exam did not go well, and she felt a heavy burden of guilt as she pedalled her cycle away from the centre. The tyres squeaked in steady rhythm, protesting the dismal start to her boards.

Her phone rang as soon as she reached home, and her mother answered it.

'Oh, it's you again. She will call you once she finishes her lunch, Riya. She just came back from the exam centre.'

Even as Kavya busied herself setting the small round dining table in the centre of their hall, she couldn't shake the feeling of terror at the thought of Riya's next call. She had stalled enough, and the girl was at the brink of her patience. What was she going to tell her anyway? Darsh had not yielded.

'I've made you your favourite dal, Kavi,' her mother said endearingly as she served her.

'You've worked hard all year. I know you're going to ace the exams.'

If only she could tell her mother how pressured she felt. This exam was her supposed way out of the town—her mother had incessantly drilled that into her. Now, she wanted to hug her and tell her she wouldn't make it. But she couldn't. She couldn't tell her about the drama surrounding Darsh. She couldn't tell her that her nerves had been frayed for quite some time. She couldn't tell her that she wasn't a brilliant student who would miraculously score ninety-nine per cent and attend St Stephen's College next year. She couldn't tell her that her daughter was just average—it would break her heart.

But average she was. She couldn't keep her promise to Riya, she couldn't convince Darsh, and she was failing at life, not just her exams.

Later that night, she fell asleep thinking about the questions she had missed, which now seemed relatively easy.

She dreamt of snow. In a white wonderland somewhere, she was laughing and jumping around with no one else in sight. She felt free. Her dream self was weightless; she could float at will and peek at clouds up close. Then, a snowball came hurtling towards her and hit her right on the head. It didn't hurt, but she fell back onto the snow with a thump. She looked around just in time to see another one approaching, and flinched to avoid it.

That's how she woke up—and saw that her window, which had been slightly ajar, was now wide open. A couple of mud balls were on the floor.

Darsh was calling.

Thirteen

The clock on her bedside table said four-thirty. His mud ball had made an appearance after quite a while. She didn't move. Meeting him during the exams would be foolish. She needed to keep her head – or whatever was left of it – clear and focused.

She climbed down from the bed and walked to the window. His bike was just under her window, and he sat on it, waiting for her. With half-open eyes, she changed into jeans and a white sweater and tied her hair into a tight ponytail. She glanced at her reflection before opening the back door that led to the stairs. Groggy eyes and hair that was already coming undone. Why did he always have to give her such short notice?

On the other hand, it was clear that he hadn't slept at all. His eyes were blank yet alert, perusing Kavya unblinkingly as she neared him. She found something peculiar about how he looked at her—as if searching for something new.

'What's wrong? You know I have another test tomorrow.'

A long breath escaped him, sounding like a sigh, as he turned and made a place for her on the bike.

'Let's go for a ride.'

'But I have an exam tomorrow.'

He didn't say anything, and she looked at the awaiting seat hesitatingly but climbed up resignedly. She knew she didn't want to go back and sleep. She couldn't go back and sleep, even if it meant failing.

He parked the bike once the pathway in the jungle narrowed down and disappeared into the undergrowth. They walked through the sea of ferns as faint morning light filtered through the dense treetops. Eventually, they walked into a small round clearing that Kavya had never seen. A near-continuous tangle of dull brown trunks blocked the view around the clearing, giving it the feel of a capsule. Stepping into it was like a time machine, an instant disconnect from the current world.

He plonked under one of the trees and stared at the sky over him. Mentally, he seemed to be in unknown territory.

She lay there a little away from him, listening to the wind whipping through the treetops, knowing she was messing with her future every minute she was here. Despite the daylight starting to creep in, the moon hung in the sky obstinately, reminding her a little bit of herself. She felt helpless that despite knowing she had a paper that she was going to screw up, she was content right now being here with him by her side. The realisation brought forth a silent trepidation. She was beyond help. She heard a bird flap its wings over them and noticed that the forest air seemed filled with a stagnant green. That's when he spoke up.

'When I went to see her, she was a tiny bag of skin and bones, mostly crying without any reason,' he said abruptly, and for Kavya, the sounds of the jungle disappeared. She sat up slowly and faced him. Was he talking about his mother?

He looked at her. His gaze was half lost and half questioning.

'So much drama is created all through life, only to die in the end, like a rotting vegetable. It's almost comical.'

Kavya opened her mouth and then closed it. What do you say to Darsh Purohit? Was he grieving? Was he sad? Or was he just bored?

'You told me there's no harm, but there was. Now, when she is dead, instead of remembering the haughty woman she was, I can only see that weak, pleading face stripped of all gravity.'

'She died? When?' Kavya's question came out in a whisper as she felt the physical shock of his words pound into her heart.

'This morning.'

Kavya hadn't known his mother well. She had seen her from afar, but they had never had a conversation. She was extraordinarily beautiful and had the same eyes as Darsh's. She also remembered her towering air and how the Purohit House staff trembled even at her name. A sweeper at his house once told her she was a strict disciplinarian and used to hit Darsh regularly. The town grapevine also held her in low regard, claiming she had never even shown affection to her son.

Tears stung her eyes from nowhere. She was feeling for Darsh because he didn't feel for himself. And she was ashamed of it, so she hid her tears by looking away.

'How's the girl? She still wants to see me?'

It took Kavya a few seconds to realise he had changed the subject, and she looked back at him blankly. 'I will meet her once if she still wants to, but you must be there too.'

'Why the change of mind?'

'I don't know, Kavya. Why does she want to meet me?'

'She thinks she is in love with you.'

'And how do you love someone when you don't know them?'

That was a logical question, and he was probably expecting a logical answer to it. Kavya weighed in, telling him that love made people behave quite illogically, but decided against it. She would not win this debate tonight, and he was not in a good mood. Perhaps a lighter response would earn her a rare smile.

'Umm ... you know that half the girls in this town are planning to marry you because you are just insanely attractive to look at? For them, it's enough.'

It made no difference to him. He picked up a stone and threw it towards some imaginary target. 'That's not very smart, is it? My father married her because of how she looked. Look how that turned out.'

She went back to being silent, not knowing how to react when he talked about his mother. At the same time, she was glad he completely disregarded physical beauty, as she considered herself very ordinary-looking.

'Love...' he said it aloud and paused as if to weigh the word, then continued, 'Fucking scam.'

'Just be nice when you let her down. I don't want her hurting herself again,' she added cautiously.

Kavya didn't sleep after coming back. There were two hours before the alarm would have gone off, but her mind was experiencing heightened activity. Darsh was upset. It was one of the rare times he was being threatened with emotions he didn't know. That caused a glitch in his otherwise emotionless thought pattern and made him agree about seeing Riya. But it was Kavya he sought when he found himself in unknown territory. He wanted her around. He wanted to share his grief with her; he didn't know how. And he did not care that she wasn't pretty. Kavya felt reassured after months. It was time to show him that love wasn't a scam at all. It was real. As real as it got.

She could hardly stay up while writing her exam. English Elective demanded descriptive answers, but she wrapped the paper in an hour and headed home. Somehow, the threat of failing lost its power over her because she felt validated by Darsh. Riya was ecstatic when she got to know, and Kavya even gave her a few suggestions about keeping her cool when facing Darsh. She was both happy and sad that she already knew the outcome of this 'meeting', and she could only hope that Riya would leave them alone after this.

Two days later, at Jeeva Lake, Kavya sat with her, shaded by a huge boulder that blocked the sparse crowd from seeing them. The lake was partially visible from this corner, and the undergrowth on the path to this spot was thick, making it ideal for secret rendezvous. Anyone approaching would be heard well before they did by the sound of rustling grass.

'Riya, if it doesn't work out, do you promise you won't harm yourself?' Kavya asked for the tenth time, to which Riya nodded impatiently. She had been all over the place for a while now despite Kavya's suggestion that she appear rational to Darsh and not crazed.

Soon, she saw him appearing at the curve, silhouetted by the portion of the lake visible from their nook. He was in his usual attire, a white T-shirt, flanked by an open shirt and blue jeans. He was also wearing a pair of sunglasses, given that they had asked him to come in the afternoon when the sun was overhead so they could meet before the place started filling up with the evening boating crowd. As a result, his face was even more unreadable as he joined them. There were no greetings, as if he expected them to get to the point immediately. Riya spoke then.

'Thanks for coming—'

'So, tell me, what's this all about?' he interrupted her, his voice flat and cold, as he removed his glasses and fixed his gaze on her. The eyes seemed even colder, hardly hiding his impatience.

Riya glanced uncertainly at Kavya and then looked back at him before lowering her eyes in confusion. She was trying to find words. Kavya felt sorry for her already. He did not seem in his best mood.

'Darsh, I love you,' Riya said abruptly, as if inspired by a sudden boldness, and then stopped. He did not react at all. There was a moment of awkward silence and then she attempted to explain.

'I can't think about anything else since the day we met. I can't even go to sleep. I think about you all the time. I have never felt like this. Please give this a chance … I want to be your friend … I mean, girl … girlfriend.'

He still didn't say anything and his expression remained unchanged. Any normal person would have shown some emotion, but Darsh wasn't normal. Yet, Kavya hoped he would be as nice as possible. He was probably weighing in on how to respond. Being in a situation like this would have killed her.

When he finally spoke, his voice came out tired, like he had already had enough of this conversation.

'Listen to me very well, Riya. Can you do that?'

She nodded hopefully.

'It's just sex. That's all you need to get this 'love' out of your system. But you are what? Fifteen? Sixteen? Too young for me to do anything about it. I'm sorry.'

It took Riya a few seconds to comprehend his shocking response. Seemingly appalled at his simplistic explanation of her feelings, she started defending herself.

'No, no, no … that's not true at all…'

'It would be statutory rape—exactly what you've been threatening to accuse me of, I hear,' he cut her off coldly.

Riya went red in the face in a matter of seconds. She opened her mouth and then closed it, at a loss for words. Her gaze shifted towards Kavya in a desperate plea to help her, but Kavya did not know what to say. Darsh chose that moment to turn around and leave, and Riya rushed to stop him in a last attempt. Kavya saw her jump in his way and grab both his hands to physically restrain him from leaving.

'Darsh, listen to me, please. I … I'm sorry. I know it was totally wrong of me, but I really needed to get your attention. Love makes you do crazy things. It's not just a physical attraction… My feelings are deeper … I can prove it … please!'

He looked down at her hands, which held his own in a tight, desperate grip, and Kavya just knew he was not going to entertain this even for a moment longer. She also knew Riya would not get closure if he just left like that. They would be back to square one, and all her persistence would mean nothing. She didn't dare interfere, but her heart was beating fast, hoping Darsh wouldn't leave. In that tiny moment, she saw him raise his eyes to her as if he knew exactly what she was thinking. She was tearing up, anticipating the failure of the exercise. She would be getting more desperate phone calls every day if he left like this.

And then, with an audible sigh of resignation, Darsh turned his attention back to Riya and stepped forward. Removing his hands from her clasp, he angled her face up towards him and placed his mouth on hers. It was chaste at first, giving her time to register, refuse, or respond. And respond she did. She lunged forward and glued herself to him. He indulged her. His mouth engulfed hers in a clean, expert move, delving deep to continue.

Kavya froze in shock. She had never seen anyone kissing except in movies, and to see him doing it to someone else did strange things to her. She felt angry yet excited. There was a sudden wetness between her legs that made her feel ashamed. Darsh raised his eyes again to look at Kavya even while Riya moaned in his mouth, but Kavya couldn't look away. She wanted to tear them apart, yet couldn't take her eyes off them. She wanted to run away, yet stayed fixed to the spot, watching them … him … hungrily.

He stopped as suddenly as he had started. When he withdrew, gently removing himself from her tight grip, Riya was a dazed mess, unable to appreciate what was happening.

He spoke in a calm, measured tone, as if his point had been proven. 'Not about sex, you were saying? That's just your body asking for more. Calling it love might make you feel better, but seeing it for what it is would be a better way out of the mess you're making for yourself.'

'Wow,' Riya whispered, still not out of it. Unsteady on her feet, she leaned on the rock behind her and ran her hand over her mouth. Her face was flushed red, and her eyes shone like she was the happiest person on the planet.

'Don't call my home, and don't bother Kavya about this anymore, okay? What just happened is not going to happen again. This is the last you'll see of me. Hurting yourself or threatening her will make me regret seeing you today. I'm sure you don't want that.'

Riya nodded eagerly, ready to agree to everything now that she did not feel wholly spurned. Her body was singing; it was impossible not to be happy at that moment. Also, she felt like she'd won—gotten him to respond in some way, even if it was just this once.

'Would ... um ... do you mind if I tell a few friends that I kissed you?' He shrugged. 'Sure, tell everyone. Doesn't matter to me.'

As he was leaving, he stopped near Kavya for a second with an I-told-you-so look. 'Just hormones. It will pass.'

With that, he disappeared around the corner, leaving two bemused girls unable to make any sense of the strange encounter. Riya should have been feeling utterly rejected, but she didn't. She was still basking in the pleasure of the unexpected kiss. Kavya was still stupefied, and they both made their way back in silence, unable to sort their feelings into clear boxes.

Fourteen

Kavya appeared in this state of knots for her following paper and the next. She was sure that she was in love with Darsh and that he was ruthless with people's feelings. Sex, that's what he thought Riya wanted. What would he say when he found out Kavya felt tenfold what Riya was feeling? And the blatant kissing she was made privy to? It didn't leave her for a single moment. She carried it everywhere—while writing her exams, reading her books, and sleeping. How did Riya feel when his lips were on hers? Just watching it did unbelievable things to her. What would it feel like to be kissed? Her emotional involvement was already taking a toll on her. It didn't help that the physical attraction was getting out of hand, too.

Her exams were finally over, and Kavya felt worse than usual on the final day. The eventuality of facing the consequences seemed nearer now. The results would be out in a while, and the world would end for her mother. You are my only daughter, she would say; you were my only hope, she would say.

Kavya carried the burden of academic performance ever since she entered school. Her mother was an ambitious woman who could not pursue her aspirations. She was married at eighteen to Kavya's father and recalibrated her life by engaging in housework and rearing her only child. All her hopes and ambitions were pinned on Kavya. If Kavya did not get into a top college in the capital city after her twelfth, it would amount to colossal failure—not just for her daughter but for her as a mother, too.

You have to get out of this town.

Academics are your only ticket.

I will see to it that you become a doctor.

But Kavya wanted romance in her life. Her parents had a dead marriage, and she always imagined hers would be different. She wanted a fairy tale that would beat the odds. She desperately wanted to believe that love moved mountains. If she could change Darsh, it would be the most remarkable testimony of winning with love. That was the only achievement she cared about.

Like fake friends who don't turn up when needed most, sleep evaded her all night as her mother's words floated in her mind. She tossed and turned, trying to think of brighter things, but there were none. Her nerves had come unstrung. Restless and anxious, she got up from the bed and looked at the clock. It was nearly four in the morning. Dawn was still to arrive, but it was lurking on the horizon, ready to shed light on her failures at any moment. The thought was suffocating, and Kavya tiptoed downstairs and got her bicycle out. She was going to take a slow ride alone around the town before everyone woke up.

In the strangely reassuring darkness, she cycled resolutely. Away from the familiar structures of her colony, out into the town. Under a sky resembling a black slate dome, the street lamps cast their sulphurous glow on wet roads. The intense chirping of crickets indicated their reluctance to give way to the morning birds. Winds whispered through the branches of the trees that lined both sides of the street. She crossed the residential blocks and rode towards the less populated part of the city. The topography flattened, and amidst a stretch of low-lying fields lay the town's cemetery.

Kavya would have crossed the area without a thought if she hadn't spotted Darsh's bike. She stopped in her tracks suddenly, even as her brakes squealed in protest. It was his, parked against the cemetery walls under a flickering street light.

He was in a cemetery. That was bizarre, even by his standards. With peaked curiosity and an underlying need to see him on such a tumultuous night, she mustered enough courage to look for him in a graves-filled ground. Taking a deep breath and shaking away the fear, she jumped the low wall. The temperature seemed to be lower on that side of the wall, and the night chill seeped through her T-shirt, even as she pressed the thick fabric closer to her body.

A vast, unkempt meadow stretched in front of her eyes. She waded through tall, wild grass that felt rough and shaggy across her bare arms, like uncombed hair. Once the grass gave way, she could make out the outlines of tombstones strewn haphazardly across the field. These dark, ominous silhouettes brought forth a strong gush of fright, reminding her of every horror movie she had ever watched. The howling wind and the rustling of the grass intensified her terror, and she realised she had to run back. But her legs wouldn't move. With great effort, she turned around on these structures and started walking back gingerly. But a distinct sound of a twig being stepped on behind her caused her to freeze in place.

'Kavya, what are you doing here?'

It was him. She exhaled sharply, colour rushing back into her face.

'You scared me.'

'What are you doing here at this hour?'

'I could ask you the same.'

'I come here all the time. Why is your voice so shaky? Are you upset?'

'I'm terrified. I'm standing in the middle of a graveyard.'

'Why? I mean, why aren't you sleeping?'

'I'm going to fail the boards, Darsh.' She finally voiced the hollow weight in her stomach that had been gnawing at her.

'It matters so much?'

'Yes! This was the twelfth board! I'm finished.'

'No. They are finished,' he said, pointing at the headstones. 'Dead people buried, wild grass growing all over them. Do you know how much they scored on their boards?'

'You're crazy.'

'You are—acting so fragile about every little thing when we're all going to end up here.'

She looked around at the scatter of stones, abandoned to nature's whim. It made her even sadder.

'We won't be buried but burnt...' she said for no particular reason.

'Yes. Sooner or later. So why cry and burn today?'

She didn't respond.

'Come. Follow me,' he said.

She trailed behind him to a clearing at the far end of the cemetery. Her eyes settled on a raised platform, like a grave without a headstone. He had a little set-up there—a jacket, his favourite book *The Stranger,* a couple of cigarettes, and a lighter. A quiet alcove among the dead. They sat, and Kavya could see the eastern sky glowing faintly. Dawn was moments away, a blush of orange already spilling across the horizon.

'You want to do a cremation in a cemetery?'

'What?'

'Yeah. Bring me some dry twigs and leaves—there's plenty over there. I'll get some from here.'

Kavya shrugged and stood. Anything to take her mind off the looming disaster felt welcome. The night had shifted; its randomness was oddly comforting. Together, they built a miniature pyre of twigs, leaves, and grass. Darsh scooped up wet mud and shaped it into something lumpy.

'We're cremating your board exams,' he said, placing it on the pyre.

'And the results,' she added.

'The fear of results,' he corrected.

'And expectations.'

She kept going, making a mental list.

'And opinions.'

'And Delhi colleges that won't take me.'

'And the pressure of doing what's right.'

He flicked the lighter on and glanced at her. 'Anything else?'

'Yes,' she said, swallowing as she looked at him from the corner of her eye. Her voice was careful now—she was crossing into guarded territory. But she needed to say it.

'Your grief ... for losing a mother you never had.'

He said nothing. But his face hardened, and his jaw clenched slightly. The lighter's flame wavered. She wondered if she had gone too far. Presuming how he felt—no one was allowed to do that. Still without a word, he lit the little pile.

A shiver ran down her spine as she watched the flames consume every insecurity she'd named. She felt, for a fleeting moment, completely free. She turned to him. Firelight flickered in his eyes as he stared into it, lost.

'Darsh?'

'Hmm?'

'Kiss me?'

He turned, his unreadable eyes locking on hers. The intensity didn't scare her. In fact, it emboldened her.

'Kiss me. Like you kissed her.'

The fire was smouldering, close to dying. Her courage would die with it. She lowered her eyes, ashamed. But then, his hand rose to her chin, turning her face toward him. Tilting her head gently, he leaned down and kissed her.

The world dissolved. It was soft and slow, more comforting than anything anyone had ever said to her. His hand rested beneath her ear, unmoving, even as his tongue deepened the kiss. He tasted like ash and smelled like smoke. After coaxing her into the kiss, he pulled back slightly, letting her explore. She pushed her tongue in further, shivering from the thrill it sent down her spine. When she pulled away to breathe, his gaze locked with hers—darker, sharper than ever before.

She kissed him again, and this time he parted her lips with urgency. The kiss intensified, tremors rippling through her. Her hands pressed against his chest as she leaned into him, holding on. He was her anchor in a spinning world. And then, just as suddenly, he began to pull away. Gently, firmly, he detached himself and began gathering his things.

'Let's go. The sun is up.'

Kavya turned towards the horizon, golden light washing over her skin. She let the moment settle deep into her bones. Watching him kiss Riya had ignited a storm inside her—but now it had stilled. Last night, she'd ridden through the dark with a tear-streaked face. Now she was riding home at dawn, smiling with unburdened joy. As she mounted her bicycle, she touched her cheek – right below the ear – where the dried mud from his hand remained.

Darsh Purohit had changed something in her forever. She was irrevocably in love with him.

Fifteen

In the following weeks, Kavya found an unexpected ally in Riya. To her friends from school, it was surprising that she now spent all her time with a junior who was not 'proper'. But contrary to what Kavya had assumed, Riya was a willing listener, and sleepovers at her place meant entire nights of private conversations centred around Darsh. She showed great interest in Kavya's anecdotes of growing up with him, even though she had dropped the idea of pursuing him after that day at Jeeva Lake.

Listening to Kavya gave her a window into Darsh's exclusive world—one not accessible to her otherwise. For Kavya, talking about him to someone who wouldn't judge her feelings was almost therapeutic. Somehow, meeting Darsh together that day had created an invisible thread between them.

During one of these sleepovers, after the caretaker had left, Riya proposed trying some alcohol. Kavya was initially reluctant, uneasy with the idea of crossing another boundary that would separate her from the 'good' girls. Still, Riya convinced her—partly by mocking her inhibitions, and partly by tapping into Kavya's hidden desire for rebellion.

The liquor was clear and, as Riya repeatedly specified, imported from Russia by her parents. Despite being harsh on her palate, Kavya downed the first drink quickly. Her head began to spin after a while, but her body felt warm and cosy.

They began watching a movie on the giant TV in the hall, snuggled under blankets on the large sofa. But after her second drink, Kavya started feeling restless—as if there were two versions of her, and one of them was trapped inside her body, clawing to get out.

'I think I'll sit on the verandah for a while. You continue,' she told Riya and wandered towards to the front entrance. She stepped onto the grassy lawn between the portico and the house's gate. Barefoot, she walked over the mossy grass, soaking in its fresh wetness, thinking of the night at the cemetery. A slight headiness overcame her as she finished the third drink, tossed the plastic glass across the lawn, and rolled her tongue over her lips.

It made her remember the smoke and ash and the warmth of his tongue inside his mouth. She sat back on the grass and sighed. She would give anything to see him right now and repeat that kiss. She wanted to talk to him about what it meant. She had just turned nineteen and couldn't pretend to be a child – or just a friend – any longer. Yes, she desired him, but it was different for her. It was love, not a crazed admiration. There was so much more between them, and his kiss had told her he felt it too. If only he could turn up somehow at that gate and take her away on a midnight ride. It would change everything. Tonight was different. She could tell him they belonged together.

'It's Darsh, I know. I can see you're not just friends.'

She was startled as Riya appeared and lowered herself to the ground beside her.

Kavya released an honest sigh. 'I wish…'

'Oh, you haven't told him how you feel? But you must!'

'Well, you saw how it turned out when you tried.'

'See, he's out of my league … older, reclusive, nothing in common. And now that some time has passed, I think he was right—it was just a crush. I liked him because he seemed so … umm … out of reach.'

Kavya could feel her head swimming under the stars she was gazing at. She felt formidable, as if she could win the world right then.

'But you…' Riya continued, 'You grew up with him. He's been so close to you, keeps looking for you in times of need … I think you're stupid not to tell him.'

'I am…' Kavya repeated, agreeing with her wholeheartedly.

'Yes. He just doesn't know that what's between you guys is love. But you do. You should tell him.'

'You are right. I think I will do it tonight.' Kavya stood up with a sudden resolve in her feet.

'Right now?' Riya asked, taken aback.

'Yes,' Kavya answered with determination. It was now or never.

When she left for his place, she couldn't shake off a feverish excitement that was new to her. Her grip on the handle and the brakes were slippery, and she almost lost her balance twice in her hurry. The roads were empty, and there was no one to notice how mad she looked, cycling vigorously like her life depended on it.

Her mind was as much in overdrive as her bicycle. There was no guarantee that he would be home. But all she could think about was how time seemed to be running out. Once the alcohol effect wore off, she would lose all this temporary courage.

The guard saw her approaching and opened the smaller side gate wordlessly, curiosity written all over his face. Once inside, she tossed her bicycle against the wall and walked impatiently to the outhouse. The lights were switched off, but the door was locked from inside. That was good. It meant he was in. She was speaking to herself in short sentences now, afraid her brain wouldn't process anything longer. She rapped the door sharply and waited. Right at this moment, she could tell him anything without worrying about how he responded or the consequences. She could chasten him for how stupid he had been by not reaching out to her. At that moment, she could tell him she loved him.

It was getting woozier inside her head now, and her eyelids felt heavier, making her unsteady on her feet. She beat loudly against the wooden door now, with an open palm, getting piqued at the delay.

He opened the door. She tried stepping in immediately, but was stopped.

'There's someone inside,' he said before stepping out and shutting the door quietly behind him.

Kavya noticed his appearance then. His hair was dishevelled, and the shirt had been put on hastily, still unbuttoned. He was staring at her with a curiosity laced with mild annoyance. She did the math then, albeit slowly. He looked like he had been disturbed. He said there was someone inside.

At that moment, all her feverish energy dissipated, and her heart shrunk like a deflating balloon. She tried to take a few steps back, away from him. She wanted nothing more than to be able to walk away with gravity, but all she managed were a few faltering steps in no direction. Just when she thought she would fall flat on the ground in front of him in further humiliation, he reached out a hand to steady her.

'You are drunk...'

This was more of an observation than a question.

She tried freeing herself from his hold, but he ignored it. His clasp around her arm tightened.

'Where do you want to go? You can't even walk.'

'Away from you,' she managed to say without slurring, continuing to struggle to free herself.

'But why are you here?' he asked.

She gave up her struggle, and he released her. Tired, she slumped on the ground as tears welled in her eyes. How did she get into this mess? Maybe she could worry about it tomorrow. She could lay right here on the grass and sleep under the stars. And then she felt herself being lifted in the air. The world began moving, and the structures around her became shaking shapes that moved up and down in her line of vision as she crossed them. She saw the mansion getting closer, a hazy blob of white. She turned her head and saw Darsh's face above her, faintly registering that he was carrying her to the main house.

Once inside, he lowered her on the bed, tucked her in and turned to go, but she started muttering incoherently.

'What?' he said, not comprehending her words.

'My bra ... too tight ... can't unhook.'

Her hands were trying to reach her back, and she was failing at something that was otherwise routine. He asked her to turn on her stomach. She turned, lay there, and then felt his hand inside her T-shirt, unhooking the clasp with ease. She wanted him to go on as his touch sent currents through all parts of her body that stung her most pleasantly. But the hand was out as soon as the task was done.

He was getting back up when she grabbed his hand to stop him from going back. Even in her disoriented state, where her brain felt fragmented while processing thoughts, she knew she didn't want him to go back to whoever was inside the outhouse. She also knew she would never have the courage to question it after today.

'Where are you going?'

'To my room. You get some sleep.'

'Darsh… why?'

'Why what?'

'Why kiss me?'

'You mean in the cemetery?'

She nodded.

'Because you asked me to. Listen, you are too drunk to make any sense. We will talk tomorrow.'

He removed her hand and got up.

'I love you.' The words escaped without her permission, but after he had walked away from her. Everything around her blurred as she fell into an alcohol-induced sleep.

Sixteen

The morning after her foolish trip to Darsh's house, Kavya sneaked out before anyone woke up. She had a splitting headache and couldn't bring herself to cycle back to Riya's place. She jumped the wall and made it to her room undetected. Fragments of the night came back to her, and she felt disgusted with herself.

Even after washing her face again and again, she couldn't rid her puffy face of the humiliation. She had exposed herself brazenly, and she wasn't even sure he had noticed. The headache persisted. The window that overlooked his room worsened her misery, so she shut and bolted it, hoping this physical act might help shut him out of her heart as well.

A few sleepless nights followed, during which she imagined him throwing mud balls at the window—asking if she was alright, following up about her visit, explaining if he had understood why she had come. But nothing happened. She felt humiliated and abandoned, fighting strong urges to open the window, scream, or jump the wall and break his door.

She had felt confused and sad before, but this was different. The misery didn't end—even weeks later. She avoided phone calls from friends, making up excuses when they rang the house. She seldom stepped out of her room and ate very little. Her mother tried to intervene from time to time – sometimes with force, other times with tenderness – but to no avail. Kavya would peck at her favourite dishes with complete apathy, prompting frustrated monologues that sent her retreating back to her room.

When forced to sit with her mother, she would cut vegetables mechanically, nodding along to conversations about an imagined future, while her mind drifted into a numbness that shielded her from the torturous reality of rejection and unrequited love. When asked what was wrong, Kavya found herself unable to respond. Despite her mother's love and concern, she knew the chasm of age would never allow her to be understood. Her mother's instinctive hatred for Darsh would only grow, and the fact that Kavya had drunk alcohol and spent the night at his place would estrange them further. Her mother would never forgive her for all the lies and transgressions.

A few days later, Kavya was asleep in the afternoon, after having taken a generous dose of cough syrup from the medicine cabinet, when her mother rapped loudly on the door, announcing a visitor. She opened it, suspicious—wondering who would visit after two weeks of ignored calls.

To her surprise, it was Riya. Kavya had quite a few friends, but none had enquired more than once. And here was this girl, with a reputation for selfishness, standing at her door.

'I was worried sick about you!' Riya exclaimed as soon as Kavya's mother left and they shut the door behind her.

'I don't feel like talking, Riya,' Kavya muttered, crawling back under her quilt, her eyelids heavy with drowsiness.

'No surprise. You've been overdosing on this cough syrup and knocking yourself out all day.' She quickly noticed the nearly empty bottle and tossed it in the dustbin.

'This will harm you, Kavya. It's worse than alcohol.'

She climbed into the bed beside her, refusing to let her escape.

'Listen,' she said, drawing the quilt aside, 'I'm not going anywhere until you get back on your feet and start acting normal.'

'I am normal,' Kavya replied weakly.

'Kavya, I know you're sad. I know it's got something to do with Darsh. Talk to me. Remember what I went through for months? I know how it feels.

'Yes, I reacted differently. I lied, I dragged you into it—but hey, it was all because I was hurting. And was I right or what, reaching out to you? Not only am I over him, but for the first time in my life, I've found a real friend.'

Kavya felt something shift inside her after weeks. It was as if Riya was trying to pry open a tiny door into her cold, dark place—and she was bringing a little light with her.

'I made a fool of myself that night,' she said, speaking about it for the first time.

Once she started, she couldn't stop. Her story poured out in detail, releasing the tears that had been dammed inside her since that night. Riya listened, held her hands, and nearly cried herself when Kavya told her that Darsh had been with someone else.

As the tears subsided and everything was out of her system, Kavya was surprised at how light she felt. Her feelings for Riya changed profoundly. The fact that she had made the effort to break through her walls had pulled her back from the cliff she had been dangling from for so long. And yes, she understood.

'You know that girl probably meant nothing, right? I have a PhD on Darsh Purohit, and I know he sleeps with whoever is willing. That list is long. The college crowd is very different, Kavya. Some of them are quite OK with one-night stands and such things,' Riya said, pulling a bottle of Coke from her bag and handing it to her. 'Here, this will change the taste in your mouth.'

'That's beside the point. I went there, and all he saw me as was a small disturbance. He made me sleep in his house and went back to her.'

'Come on, Kavya. What do you expect from him? You told me he doesn't understand emotions. It's your job to help him figure out what he feels for you. You can't do that in one night, and certainly not when drunk.'

'No, thank you. See that window over there? It's been bolted since that day. He is out of my life.'

'Even better, then. It's time to celebrate. When you come to my house next, we'll have a drink to that.'

They laughed a little and gulped down the rest of the Coke. Kavya realised she had been missing this kind of friendship all her life. She had always needed someone she could talk to, someone who would make the effort to reach her. Growing up in Darsh's shadow had not only deprived her of love but of friendship too. As if reading her thoughts, Riya offered her hand for a formal shake.

'From now on to forever, I am your best friend.'

She was just starting to feel better when the board results arrived. She had thought it wouldn't make any difference to her, having already hit rock bottom, but she was wrong. Hell broke loose at home when her parents saw she had barely scraped into the first division. Her mother was inconsolable. Her father sat silently in a corner, casting her a look of absolute regret. In her already broken state, their disappointment became unbearable. She cried quietly while her mother railed at her for having failed to make anything of herself.

That night, when her father left for his shift and her mother finally fell asleep, Kavya slipped out quietly, heading straight for the dam on her bicycle.

The water below roared as she stopped midway across the bridge. During the day, the bridge bustled with traffic, connecting the old and new parts of town. Even at this time of night, someone could pass by and spot her, but it seemed unlikely. Who would be crossing at two in the morning?

Juxtaposed with the silence of the night, the river's protest at being restrained seemed louder than usual. Kavya understood its frustration. She had spent nineteen years restraining herself, holding back her freer self, suppressing her feelings and trying to live up to what was expected of her. All she had known was fear: fear of disappointing her parents, of not being liked, of not being loved, of making the wrong choices. She raised her eyes to the surrounding hills, grey silhouettes against a dark starry sky. They seemed to extend a seductive invitation to break free of all boundaries and chase the lofty heights of freedom.

At that moment, she shed her fears with finality and looked down at the angrily gushing water. She was going to jump. All this insufferable pain, the humiliation, the fear, and the insecurity would end for good. Perhaps there was a heaven beyond those hills that would free her of this hopelessness. She reached for the dupatta hanging loosely over her shoulders, intending to blindfold herself. Falling into darkness would be easier than falling into those raging waves.

But her thoughts were interrupted by a faint humming sound growing louder. She turned and saw the outline of a motorbike approaching fast from the other side of the bridge. Who would be heading towards the old town at this hour? Kavya had a sinking feeling that she knew exactly who it was, and the realisation chilled her. As if caught in the act of a crime, she threw the dupatta down onto the road and froze. The spell was broken. The bike slowed down as it reached her, then came to a halt beside her.

As Darsh killed the engine, the sounds of the night returned to her, as if her life had been unpaused and the world was in motion again. Tears welled up in her eyes, and her cheek flushed with the realisation of what she had almost done. She opened her mouth, but nothing came out.

She saw him scrutinise her, then glance at the incriminating dupatta lying in a crumpled pool at her feet. She knew it would take him only seconds to figure out what she had been about to do. Her mind scrambled for a plausible explanation but gave up, overwhelmed by adrenaline.

'You were going to jump,' he said slowly, almost to himself.

She started sobbing. She couldn't tell if it was disappointment or relief that swamped her, forcing her to let go of her stoic resistance. All she knew was that the tears would not stop anymore. As the sobs turned into a full-blown crying episode, he climbed down from the bike.

He stood beside her for a few minutes, as though waiting for her to stop, but said nothing. When she didn't, he gently reached out for her hand, snaking his fingers through hers. As his unsure grip held her, she turned abruptly and hugged him tightly.

He had saved her life. If he had arrived a minute later, she would have been gone. His presence felt like a sign from the heavens, proof that her love for him was not misplaced. An avalanche of gratitude held her fast to him. He stood still like a tree as she clung to him.

'You failed the boards?' he asked when she calmed down and let him go.

Can't you see, Darsh? she wanted to scream. *It's you. You push me to the edge ... and then you pull me back. You are my punishment ... and you are my reward. Can it get sicker than that?*

'I passed, but scored the lowest in the first division,' she replied.

'And your parents probably told you the world has ended for you.'

'I've let everyone down.'

'Have you let yourself down?'

'Yes. What's the fucking point of life?'

'There is no fucking point to life. We exist, that's it. It's foolish to keep trying to find a purpose or make something of it. That's the root of all this stuff you feel.'

'You don't understand. You never will,' she said.

He ignored her interruption and, for once, spoke more words than usual.

'Look around. The wind, the trees, the hills, the lake—it's so fucking beautiful. They were exactly the same before your exams and would have stayed the same after you jumped from this bridge. Nothing matters in this universe. All the misery is just in your head.'

It was classic Darsh. He identified more with the trees and hills than with people.

'Kavya, this moment is all there is. Don't ask anything of it, just be.'

Seventeen

Trisha woke up with a headache. She had had a little too much wine again. But this time, it wasn't just regret she woke up with—it was panic.

Had she kissed Darsh Purohit? Kavya's complicated friend? The one who seemed like the human incarnation of an iceberg, with ninety per cent of his past with Kavya submerged in obscurity? Was Kavya going to be angry with her? Had he already told her?

Your horny friend came on to me while I was just waiting for a driver...

Oh no. She had to tell her before he did.

She reached for her phone in haste, knocking her alarm clock off the nightstand in the process. But she stopped midway, realising she couldn't just call and blurt something like that. She was in trouble. She had put both her job and her friendship in serious jeopardy. She needed to meet Kavya and explain, before she heard it from him.

Once at the office, she went straight to Kavya's cabin, preparing a speech that would absolve her completely. She would downplay the attraction, promise to stay away from him—anything to undo last night.

But when she entered, Kavya didn't look up or greet her like she usually did. Sitting against her large desk with the backdrop of buildings gleaming through the window, Kavya suddenly reminded Trisha of their hierarchical difference. She often forgot that Kavya was at the top of the food chain while she was at the bottom. No one reached Kavya without going through her secretary—yet Trisha had always had the privilege of walking in whenever she wanted. She had put all of that on the line yesterday.

Did she already know?

Was she being deliberately ignored?

Trisha sat down like a nervous candidate waiting to be interviewed and cleared her throat to draw attention.

'Just a minute, Trisha,' said Kavya in a measured tone, leaving her even more unsure.

When she finally looked up, Trisha wasted no time. She confessed to the events of the night before, trying to weave in a justification and an apology that came out muddled and ineffective.

To her surprise, Kavya laughed.

Was it genuine amusement, or an attempt to disguise a wave of fury on the verge of eruption?

'Relax, Trisha. It's OK,' she said, then added dismissively, 'although I don't see why you'd want to entangle yourself with someone you hardly know.'

'You know me. I'd want exactly something like that. But seriously—you're actually cool with this?'

'Why wouldn't I be? He's just a childhood friend.'

'I keep picking up a vibe, though…'

'There's nothing. Zilch.' Kavya made a big zero with her thumb and index finger, as if to drive the point home.

Trisha got the impression she didn't want their equation discussed again.

'OK, great!' she said, genuinely relieved, regaining her excitement about Darsh.

'You know, he told me his therapist in the US kept advising him to see you again, so you two must have been thick at some point ... but—'

Kavya looked up from her laptop. Her expression softened.

'He was in therapy?'

'For years, during college. And it helped. That's why he chose to do what he does now.'

For the first time since Darsh had returned, Kavya felt a faint tug of empathy. She had always known he needed fixing in the past, but learning that he had recognised it – and done something about it – cast him in a new light. She had been ghosting him, still nursing the wounds of a past that hurt. But what if he had come back not just for closure, but to free them both? Maybe she had been so busy fortifying her guard that she hadn't allowed him a chance to explain.

If what he had told Trisha was true, then his coming back wasn't an accident.

Maybe it was time to let him speak.

Once Trisha left, she gave in to the impulse and texted him about having dinner that evening—a quiet white flag. He promptly accepted.

That evening, as she stood in her kitchen wondering whether to cook or order in, he surprised her by arriving early.

'I was so scared you'd change your mind that I cancelled all my appointments and rushed home. So, what shall we cook?'

Feeling generous and forgiving was easy when he was not around, but all her nerves seemed to string themselves tight the moment he was.

'We'll just order some Chinese…' Her voice came out gruff.

'Absolutely not. Give me twenty minutes, and I'll make you the best pasta you've ever had,' he said, brimming with enthusiasm as he went into his room to freshen up. When he returned to the kitchen, Kavya caught the scent of aftershave, fresh from the shower. A crisp white shirt and cream corduroys had replaced the formals he had come home in, and his hair was still wet and tousled. He whistled cheerfully as he put on a cooking apron.

'Just help me out with finding things. I'll manage the cooking.'

True to his word, he whipped up a scrumptious-looking pasta in no time while Kavya set the table, growing more uneasy with each passing minute.

They ate and attempted to talk. Kavya found her anxiety heightening when she realised she had let her guard down by inviting him over. She felt the need to disguise her discomfort and, in a desperate attempt to appear unaffected, blurted out the first thing that came to mind.

'So, Trisha told me she kissed you.'

'She was just drunk. Tell her not to freak out about it,' he replied casually. It was clear he hadn't attached any importance to it. So that hadn't changed. Physical intimacy still meant nothing to him.

'She is freaking out. She has quite a thing for you, in case you haven't noticed.'

He paused and looked at her knowingly.

'You still feel so responsible for how others feel, Kavya? Is this a way to deflect attention from yourself?'

The accuracy of the observation unnerved her further. She pretended to focus on her food and avoided looking at him for the next five minutes. To add to her discomfort, all this talk of kissing reminded her of the only time they had kissed. She toyed with her fork, struggling to push the memory aside. He had tasted like smoke—sweet and bitter at the same time. Even all the smoking he had done in his younger days had somehow added to his desirability in that foolish phase of hers.

Suddenly, it struck her that she hadn't seen him smoke at all since his return. It seemed like a safe topic to talk about—something neutral, without emotional risk. She attempted to resume their awkward chat.

'You've quit smoking? You were rather fond of it back then.'

He seemed surprised by the question. He didn't respond immediately, but she saw his face turn pensive, as if his thoughts had drifted far away. So even this topic had failed.

'Darsh?'

'Yes. Let's just say one thing led to another,' he said at last, but didn't elaborate.

Silence returned to the table. The conversation wasn't flowing, despite her efforts. Darsh didn't seem to mind, but to her, the awkwardness felt like a failed adventure—something she blamed herself for. He had dropped everything to come home, cooked for her, and tried to break the impasse after she had invited him, and now she was ruining it. It wasn't the first time she had felt like this, but feeling it again, after more than a decade, was strange.

This feeling of inadequacy around him had been her constant companion back in Parvatnagar, but she had dismissed it then as adolescence. The sudden resurgence of that younger self, a direct result of calling this truce and letting him in, was a dangerous development.

'Let's go for a drive,' he announced suddenly, as they got up to clear the table.

'No,' she replied instinctively.

'Come on, Kavya. You know I can't chat under a concrete roof. I need open spaces, forests, greens. Come with me.'

'Where?'

'Just put on your running shoes and we'll see. I've been exploring.'

There was no motorbike anymore, but as she handed over her car keys and he took the wheel, a nagging voice inside her asked if she was once again giving him the control he used to have over her for all those years. He seemed unaware of her inner conflict, flashing her an easy smile from time to time as they drove to his destination.

After about an hour of driving, punctuated with small talk, he made a turn just before the city airport. The area was just beginning to develop, still fringed with dense, untouched forest.

He had insisted on trekking shoes, and once they stepped into the forest, Kavya knew what he had in mind. He must have found a clearing or a stream deep within and wanted to take her there, just like in the old days.

But there was something he didn't know. Kavya had not set foot near a forest since that night. Her fear of darkness still impaired her ability to move, even now. But she couldn't tell him that.

Her discomfort had been rising for some time, and now it seemed she would come undone.

Breathe, Kavya, breathe. He can't know. You will be fine.

As they made their way in, Darsh leading the trail, she tried her best to keep her eyes fixed on him. The tall wall of trees felt sinister, as if ready to swallow them whole, angry at the trespassing. It unnerved her not to know what lay behind her. She could turn and see nothing, yet imagine a hundred things hiding behind the thick trunks that dissolved into mute darkness.

Her entire body was impossibly tense. All her energy went into warding off the panic attack that loomed close. They had grown rarer over the years, and she had believed herself past them. But in this moment, engulfed by dense vegetation and cut off from civilisation, she felt powerless to stop it.

Her brain slipped into survival mode, already deciding between fight and flight if something happened. Suddenly, her chest tightened, her legs began to tremble, and she dropped to her knees in an attempt to steady herself. Her ears rang, her vision blurred, and uncontrollable sobs shook her body. She dropped her head between her legs, trying to drown out the ringing, to shut off the pain.

This will pass, she repeated to herself, but her breath quickened dangerously. The forest had triggered her severely, and she wished desperately for her medication. A fear of dying right here took over as her chest grew tighter and tighter.

Then, the ringing in her ears began to fade, and Darsh's voice reached her.

'You are OK, Kavya. I'm right here. You can hear me, right?'

His voice was calm and steady.

'I know what you're going through is scary, but it's not dangerous. Concentrate on your breathing. I'm right here.'

She did just that. She began counting her breaths, just as she had during past episodes when the attacks were frequent and brutal. He was here. He hadn't left her. Her brain, caught somewhere between past and present, started releasing surges of oxytocin, and slowly, she began to calm down.

'Think of something that makes you feel safe—your plants: the lilies, the roses, the marigolds.'

Her garden flashed before her mind's eye. The scent of the forest was replaced with the fragrance of her flowers, further relaxing her. She raised her head and looked at him. When he noticed she was coming out of it, he reached for her hand. She lunged forward and hugged him tightly, overcome with relief that he was there.

He no longer felt like an immovable tree, as he had when they were younger, but like a warm human being whose arms wrapped back around her in genuine response. They stayed like that for a while—Kavya still on her knees, and he crouched beside her, their arms wound tightly around each other. After a few minutes, she let go, as full awareness returned.

Exhausted from experiencing such a severe attack after more than a decade, she lay on the ground and let the tears flow. Darsh lay beside her in silence. It felt almost like one of their treks into the Parvatnagar jungle, when no words were needed.

It puzzled her—the way her body had reached for him like that, when even the slightest accidental contact with others usually made her recoil. She hadn't experienced the warmth of an embrace in over ten years. It reminded her of the safety she felt when potting plants, her hands buried deep in the soil, anchoring vulnerable seeds. Fresh tears slid down her cheek as she realised how cold her life had become.

And yet—hadn't this aversion taken root because of him? Then how could his touch make her feel so safe now?

She was both confused and afraid of what this meant.

'Can we go back now?' she muttered in a hoarse voice, eyes still on the moonless sky.

'Yes, of course,' he said.

On the way back, Kavya slept like a baby. After years of watching her own back, scanning for danger in everything around her, a considerable part of that lifelong fear and distrust had been washed away with the tears she shed in the middle of the foreboding forest.

Eighteen

Trisha was glad Kavya remained unperturbed after her confession. Her indifference seemed genuine, relieving Trisha of the nagging guilt she had been carrying about liking Darsh. Her college friends would have labelled him a 'package' right away. Outside of looking so dreamy, he exuded an easy charm in his demeanour that was difficult to resist.

He seemed like an open book, yet had a shroud of mystery carefully wrapped around him. The way he hadn't resisted her kiss, yet did nothing to encourage it had fascinated her even more. She was tired of bouncing from one relationship to another. Her love life was a trail of disappointments, and she knew with certainty that someone like Darsh would never cross her path again. He probably had eight or more years on her, as he was older than Kavya, but the considerable age gap made him even more appealing. She needed tenured shoulders to rest her spontaneous head on.

With someone like him, though, the general dating rules wouldn't apply. He had already snubbed her advances that night, even if very nicely. She needed to ask him outright if he planned to stay long, and if he had a girlfriend. She needed to discuss her *modus operandi* with Kavya. He was too good a chance to lose because of her out-of-control impulses.

When Trisha presented her questions to Kavya the next day at her home, Kavya got an inkling of how serious her friend was. This knowledge produced mixed feelings. She wanted to protect Trisha from the heartbreak that was always a certainty when playing with Purohit. Still, she didn't want to be seen as jealous when all she felt was a slight discomfort—probably because of the weirdness of the situation.

Then, there was the strange encounter in the forest. However hard she tried to shrug it off as a coincidence, the fact that her body had not rejected Darsh's touch had left her feeling very unsettled.

She had convinced herself that she was quite satisfied with the way things were and that she did not, in fact, want to be touched. Years ago, in business school, when she had first realised how strong her aversion was, she had visited a doctor who termed her 'condition' something called haphephobia before referring her to a psychiatrist. Being diagnosed had felt like an insult to her younger self, and she never followed up after that one visit. It was easier to maintain that it was just one of her quirks—and that she didn't want it any other way.

But the forest visit with Darsh had challenged her years of conditioning. Somewhere inside her, a vague hope had begun to germinate—the possibility of being normal again.

'So, Kavya, what would make him take me seriously? I know he doesn't, but I want him to—really badly,' Trisha insisted, pulling Kavya back to the present.

They were sitting on Kavya's couch on a lazy Saturday afternoon without Darsh. He had left on Friday for a talk in a neighbouring city. Kavya handed Trisha a large cup of green tea, refusing to serve alcohol in the afternoon. Her friend's earnestness in trying to woo Darsh reminded her of the past. Even after all these years, he was as irresistible as ever. It was just that Kavya was immune now—in the way that, once you get burnt in a fire, you learn how important it is to keep your distance, even if it dances seductively before your eyes.

'My advice is, don't take him seriously. He might be gone tomorrow, next week, or next month. He doesn't even know his plans.'

'You're not being helpful.'

'I'll be honest with you, Trish. I know how you feel. He's had that effect on everyone for as long as I can remember—but you have to trust me when I say he's not worth it.'

'Tell me why you feel so, or let me judge him on my own.'

'I've known him all my life. Isn't that enough for you?'

'You *knew* him, Kavya. Years ago. You don't know him now. People change.'

Kavya thought about that. Could someone like him change fundamentally? He could put up an act for the world—but what was he like behind closed doors? Was empathy innate, or could it be cultivated?

'Well, what do you want from me?'

'Help me give this a serious shot.'

'Dropping hints won't get you anywhere with him. Tell him you're interested, ask him out, and see how it goes.'

'Exactly what I was thinking,' Trisha said. 'How long is he gone for?'

'A couple of days, he said. So you've got some time to change your mind.'

After Trisha left, buoyant at having gained her friend's approval, Kavya decided to make a long-pending call. She had been avoiding her mother's calls for a couple of weeks after a spat, but this Darsh-free weekend gave her the space to think. She had been furious when a matrimonial profile had been created for her without her consent on a website. The argument had escalated when her mother gave her number to some 'suitable matches'.

Receiving unsolicited calls from strangers at her mother's behest had driven her to a screaming match. Sometimes she felt her mother was the most irrational person on earth. And yet, her heart would soften when she remembered how crucial her mother's support had been during the worst phase of her life. Tonight, she decided to call her and end the fight—not because she expected anything different from her on the subject of marriage, but out of a sense of gratitude.

When she had lived at home, her parents had hounded her to 'make something of herself', and now that she had, they were hounding her to get married. It seemed nothing could satisfy her mother. *I wish you were the kind of person who could be happy alone, but you're not. That's why I worry*. That was always the justification for the pestering.

Was her mother right to assume she was unhappy? Kavya didn't know anymore. Before Darsh had returned out of nowhere, she had felt so distant from her past that she had genuinely started believing she was happy. But now, things were getting complicated again.

'Hi, Maa. Sorry for shouting at you last time and not picking up. I've been swamped,' she began as soon as the call connected.

'Leave all that. Did you talk to any of those guys?'

Kavya gritted her teeth but kept her voice calm. 'No. And I won't talk to random guys picked off a matrimonial site.'

'Then find someone, no, Kavya? I know you'll never get married if I leave it to you.'

'And why is that such a bad thing?'

'Don't pretend it's your choice to be alone. Don't put on an act for me. You don't want to spend your life alone. I know that.'

'I do, actually. People change. I've grown up.'

There was a pause on the other end, as if her mother were weighing her words. Then she approached the dreaded subject.

'Are you still affected by what happened? It doesn't matter, Kavya.'

Kavya didn't know what to say. She hung up, livid at how casually her mother had brought up that night.

Nothing happened that night.

Nineteen

Feeling slightly agitated after hanging up, Kavya busied herself cleaning the house. It was too hot to sit outside with the plants, and her maid hadn't turned up—something she didn't mind. Cleaning always helped calm her mind, second only to tending her terrace garden. The steady hum of the vacuum cleaner drowned out the cacophony in her head, soothing her nerves.

She was successful, envied by her peers, and well known in her hometown—but that was never enough for her mother. Why was it so difficult for her to understand, especially when she knew Kavya's situation? Meeting strangers via an online portal and relaying her personal history wasn't exactly an enticing prospect. What kind of marriage would survive if one partner didn't want to be touched?

Kavya had long convinced herself that relationships weren't meant for her—not with her intimacy issues. But the surprising exception of that evening when she had hugged Darsh continued to unsettle her. After years of flinching at even hand-holding or a quick peck on the cheek, the comfort his proximity brought was baffling—more so because her mind was always on edge around him.

She had avoided going into the downstairs room for a long time. But with him out of town, she finally entered to clean up. The room, however, was already immaculate. For the hundredth time, Kavya wondered how a person could transform so completely. She remembered how unkempt his outhouse room used to be—an intentional rebellion against his mother's obsession with order.

Now, if not for the thick stack of books on the nightstand, she wouldn't have known anyone lived there. Curious, she opened his closet, expecting a chaotic mess. Instead, rows of ironed clothes hung neatly, perfectly arranged. The scent of his perfume lingered in the air, a quiet reminder that she was trespassing. She was about to shut the door when her eyes fell on a set of files. Ignoring her conscience, she pulled them out.

They appeared to be a collection of his academic records—an endless series of accolades, gold medals, honorary degrees, distinctions, and invitations from prestigious institutions, all filed with meticulous care. What an extraordinary brain he had! It reminded her of the time he had scored the highest in the board exams, yet insisted on studying at the local college just to provoke his father.

But at the end of the stack, something unexpected caught her eye: a printed email exchange. It was Darsh's resignation letter from the Department of Psychiatry at UCSF. He had written of his intention to return to India permanently and requested termination. The resignation had been accepted.

Kavya read it twice to be sure she wasn't imagining things. He had quit his job and come back to India—for good. Why had he hidden this from her?

She replaced the papers where she'd found them and returned to her room, suddenly feeling lightheaded. She lay down for a while, her mind whirring.

Had she been fooling herself about being in control of the situation? Like an ostrich with its head in the sand, she had chosen to ignore the fact that his return was deeply disruptive. But perhaps it was time to confront the truth. He was here, living in her house, charming her only friend, coaxing her to let down her guard, and slowly turning her life from a quiet, manageable routine into something layered and unpredictable. Worse, his purpose remained completely unclear.

The old Darsh—detached and brutally honest—had at least been transparent because he didn't care. Kavya found herself wondering if that version had been easier to deal with than this warm, enigmatic man who kept important parts of himself hidden.

But then, perhaps he had no hidden agenda at all. Was the kindness and comfort he offered something worth dissecting—or just a natural outcome of his evolution over the years? Maybe she was just a pause, a pit stop, before he found his real destination. Perhaps he had chosen Bangalore for its hospital networks and the growing mental health landscape, just as he claimed.

But what if he hadn't? What if he had returned with the assumption that she would still go weak in the knees around him, that she would surrender control all over again? What if he was here to quietly reclaim her life and reduce her to the obscure, self-doubting girl she used to be?

She felt sweat bead on her forehead, despite the fan spinning overhead. The anxiety was creeping in again.

Since deciding to make peace with him, she had begun experiencing bouts of nervousness. That full-blown panic attack in the forest—the one she had no control over—had been her first in years.

She was playing with fire by letting him back in.

It was time to set things straight, she told herself, with finality.

He arrived late at night, and Kavya was sitting at the dining table when the key turned in the door. Choosing to end the hide-and-seek game he had started was the hardest thing she had done in years.

He stepped in quietly and closed the door behind him, unaware of her presence. As he parked his suitcase and started walking towards his room, his eyes fell on her, and he seemed taken aback.

'You scared me! Why aren't you sleeping?' he said.

'I wanted to talk to you … urgently,' she replied, her face impassive, ignoring the pleasant sensation that ran through her at the sight of him after two days.

His expression softened with concern. Kavya couldn't get over how a face that used to reveal so little in his younger days had now become so readable—unless even that was a lie.

'Of course,' he said, drawing out the chair opposite hers and sitting down. Only the hanging light directly above them was on, casting the table in the solemn aura of an inquisition.

Kavya drew a long breath and asked, 'Why are you here, Darsh? I know there's more to it than your talks, seminars, and networking.'

He didn't answer immediately. To fill the silence, she laid her cards on the table.

'I know you've left the US for good. I saw your resignation letter.'

'Oh,' he said, leaning back in his chair, running a tired hand through his hair.

A full minute seemed to pass before he offered anything further.

'Kavya, I'm sorry you found out before I could tell you. I know how this must feel...'

He paused again. Though his eyes didn't leave hers, they seemed to drift into a faraway space—lost in thoughts she couldn't access. Before she could challenge the silence, he continued.

'I didn't mean to hide anything. We just never had the chance to talk.'

'Then talk now,' she said, growing more suspicious with every passing second.

She saw it then—a flicker of serious intent in his expression, as though he were about to confess something monumental. But it vanished quickly, and his voice came out casual.

'I'd been thinking about coming back for a while. The hospital set-up just wasn't for me. Too many problems...'

'Like?'

'The system. I had ideas, but the hierarchy and politics were stifling. And there was always this need to justify a position I never even wanted in the first place.'

'Because you were a foreigner?' she asked, genuinely curious. She had never allowed him to open up before—

never truly listened. It was the first time the spotlight was on him.

'I don't know … maybe because I was younger than most? Anyway, long story short—I wasn't happy in a system that dulled my … how do I put it … spirit?'

'Yeah, that part I know,' she interjected. It was beginning to sound like the kind of conversation they should have had earlier. If only things between them hadn't been so tangled for so long. Kavya realised, with some surprise, that she genuinely wanted to know more about his life—if only to silence the disquieting doubts that cropped up every other day.

'My priorities have changed, Kavya,' he said.

'How so?'

'I'm no longer chasing a great career or trying to do this professionally.'

'Meaning?'

'I'm exploring the idea of setting up a facility in India—something geared towards teens and young adults, something they can actually afford. Deciding to seek help for mental health is hard enough; they shouldn't have to worry about paying for it.'

'What's made you so … philanthropic?' she asked, the derision in her tone barely concealed.

'Kavya, first let me say—I'm glad we're talking,' he said warmly, catching the edge in her voice but not reacting to it. 'Let me continue over some strong black coffee,' he added, getting up to switch on the kettle.

'You remember when we were kids? Everyone knew I was wrong in the head—except me. I keep wondering: if my father, or anyone really, had said I needed help, wouldn't my first twenty-five years have been different?'

He leaned against the kitchen counter, facing her, as the kettle began to boil.

Kavya stiffened.

'They all talked behind my back, but no one said a word to my father. No one ever suggested I needed therapy. Maybe a teacher could've stepped in. But all I got was either adulation from kids who saw me from a distance, or contempt from parents who saw me as trouble. I never knew anyone who looked at me and thought—here's someone who could be better. Who could try.'

He carried two steaming mugs, placed one in front of her, and took his seat again. Taking a long, relaxed sip from his own mug, he said quietly, 'Except you.'

'Don't,' she said, almost reflexively, feeling a familiar unease rise within her.

'I'm just saying you saw me. I realised it much later, but I think being around you kept me redeemable.'

This was exactly what she feared. She wasn't ready for this. All the blood drained from her face; she didn't know how to stop the conversation from treading dangerous ground.

'I'm also aware that being around me affected you in the worst ways,' he added, even more softly.

'I don't want you to talk about it,' she said, finding her voice. She noticed a slight tremor in her leg.

'I'm not,' he said, steering the conversation firmly back to himself. 'I'm talking about my own issues—undiagnosed ones. I was medically diagnosed with

PTSD in the US. It manifested as a complete absence of empathy for a quarter of my life. Can you imagine the years lost just because I couldn't get myself sorted?'

'I can very well imagine,' she said aloud, her voice trembling. The past was already flooding back, despite her forbidding herself from going there. His lost years had cost her far more than anyone else.

He must have sensed her discomfort because he stood up and walked over to her side. Sliding between the table and her chair, he perched on the edge of the table and took her hands in his. Intertwining his fingers with hers, he stared down at their joined hands without saying a word. The silence was jarring, but the tremor in her leg stopped as his warmth seeped into her cold hands.

This was black magic, she thought. How did he still have this effect on her with just a touch?

He looked up, and their eyes met. He raised his other hand and touched her face. Without thinking, Kavya leaned into him and buried her head in his shirt. With her face hidden, she allowed herself to melt into this rare comfort of physical warmth. But a moment later, a vaguely familiar sensation stirred within her—one she hadn't fully understood years ago. Her heart fluttered for a second, as if she were nineteen again.

Confused and scared, she looked up at him, her eyes searching his for answers.

He stared back at her. The intensity on his face made him look almost vulnerable, which was rare. She had the impulse to raise her hand and smooth the lines on his forehead. But then she saw it—the mask coming back down. His face changed. He let go of her and stood up, returning to his seat and his coffee.

After a long pause, he spoke again.

'Kavya, I'm sorry for pushing you to go to the forest with me that night.'

So, he was thinking about her episode in the forest. The mention made her uneasy. She didn't want to revisit it. Nothing came out of her mouth.

'So, I was thinking… why don't we go out on a proper date? To a nice restaurant?' he said from across the table, his tone casual again.

'Why?'

'What do you mean why? I'm asking you out.'

Twenty

Although she told him she would think about it, Kavya was certain she didn't want to go out with Darsh. It would have been a dream come true at twenty, but now she was a different woman. And then there was Trisha, with her plans of asking him out. Kavya needed to discourage her again. If Darsh was asking her out, then Trisha was headed for rejection.

When she woke up and came downstairs the following day, Darsh was out running as usual. She felt relieved that a text saying *no* would be enough to get her off the hook, sparing her a fumbling face-to-face explanation.

But just as she approached her car, she saw him enter through the gate. He was dressed in grey joggers and a round-necked white T-shirt. Thanks to the sweat from his run, the fabric clung to his torso. Even in his early youth, he had towered over most people with his tall frame. Back then, he would slump over like a brooding figure, but now his shoulders were broader, his body leaner, and his face seemed to glow with its own inner light.

He removed his earphones as they met near the car and gave her an impossibly cheerful smile.

'Good morning, Kavya. Leaving already? I was thinking of fixing you breakfast.'

She stared up at him. His cheeks were flushed from the run, and his eyes glowed a warm, sunlit brown. Something deep within her stirred again. She remembered that dull throb inside her when she had watched him stealthily in his kitchen that night twelve years ago, minutes before he had extinguished all her desire for him.

'Running late for a meeting,' was all she managed before climbing into her car.

She couldn't understand what was happening to her since yesterday. If she didn't know better, she would have thought she was beginning to feel physically attracted to him—but that couldn't be. In over a decade, she had never felt aroused, not even while watching an erotic film or reading a steamy novel. Even the *idea* of sex made her nauseous. And yet, he had touched her several times, and her body had welcomed it. And now, she wondered what would happen if he touched her *differently* someday.

All this confusion worked her up by the time she reached the office. She sent him a curt message:

'Can't do dates, sorry.'

An hour later, during a meeting, his reply flashed on her screen:

'It's all right. A guy had to try :)'

He even handled rejection better than she did. Was there anything he didn't excel at? Thankfully, she had a packed schedule and was able to put it aside as the day progressed. She even forgot to warn Trisha about not asking him out and was caught off guard when she received a message from her that evening:

'Have been trying to see you, but you seem busy. He said yes! We're going out tonight! Yay.'

The gnawing feeling from the morning came rushing back as she read the message. A wave of disappointment hit her, and she searched for a reason throughout the drive home. Was it because she had expected better from him? It was wrong of him to lead Trisha on if he wasn't genuinely interested. She knew he wasn't—he had asked her out just the night before. Was Darsh Purohit simply looking for a fling with whoever was available? Was she just anyone to him—easily replaced by Trisha the moment she said no?

Her mind drifted back to what Riya had once told her—that he would sleep with anyone in town, as long as it remained purely physical. What if he was treating Trisha the same way? What if he looked at Kavya the same way? Why had she thrown herself at him in the forest that night? Why had it felt so good to be in his arms?

The thought upset her so much that she was nearly shaking by the time she unlocked her front door. The emptiness of her house seemed to mock her. Trisha's message had triggered her in a way she hadn't anticipated. She could feel all her carefully built control slipping.

Kavya sank to the floor, doing everything she could to stop herself from crying, even as sweat began to bead on her forehead. She was having an episode—right here, in her own house, her only place of refuge. What was happening to her? What had Darsh done to her?

Fear gripped her chest. Clutching at the centre of her ribcage, she made a dash for the kitchen cabinet, grabbed her medication, and washed it down with a glass of water—just in time.

Slumped on the sofa, she hated herself for feeling so weak again. *A crazy woman who needed pills just to fucking survive*. She was furious—with herself, with him, with Trisha. Last night, when they had sat close together, she had instinctively felt she could trust him. There had been a connection forming—she was sure of it.

But clearly, it had all been in her head.

Darsh hadn't returned as a reformed, gentler person. He hadn't changed. He didn't care about her feelings. Her mind had been playing cruel games, luring her back towards another fall.

She had spiralled downward, and there was no point resisting anymore. She got up and opened the cabinet above the kitchen counter to retrieve the two bottles of vodka she hadn't touched in months. Her no-drinking-at-home rule felt like a relic from another life. The present now belonged to this out-of-control, worthless wretch of a woman who didn't deserve self-care.

She drank straight from the bottle and loved the way the clear liquid scorched her throat on the way down. She wanted it to hurt. She deserved it—for daring to hope again. As she finished one bottle, her foggy mind urged her to take a few more pills as well. She went to get them, knocking over the empty bottle on the way. It shattered into jagged shards on the floor.

Lying there – vodka in her veins, two pills swallowed – her eyelids began to grow heavy. The fan on the ceiling appeared and disappeared as her vision flickered. It was an antique fan with five blades—an absurdity against her otherwise modern ceiling, fitted with LED lights that, mercifully, were turned off. In the faint yellow light filtering from a lone bulb in the kitchen, her gaze fixed on the glinting gold embellishment on the fan hub. Grotesque. Why had she bought this? Because she was stupid and utterly clueless.

She had imagined she'd figured life out over the years. But every day, she'd made foolish decisions—like buying that fan. Like allowing Darsh to swoop back in and ruin her life all over again.

The thoughts soon gave way to a strange calm. Numbness crept in, and she welcomed it hungrily—but it arrived in waves. From time to time, a dull ache jabbed through her head and neck, dragging her back. She got up and took another gulp from the second bottle. Her body felt like it was on fire. She peeled off her clothes so her skin could revel in the cold marble floor. Curling into a ball, she picked up a piece of the broken bottle.

The long knife from years ago flashed across her mind. Her life could end now, and she would welcome it—gladly.

That was her last thought before slipping into unconsciousness.

Twenty-One

She woke up in her bed, disoriented and parched. The ceiling indicated it was her room, and so did her bed cover. She was wearing a large men's T-shirt, which she hadn't seen before. She rolled her tongue over her dry lips, her mouth tasting of metal. The bile in her stomach rose alarmingly fast, and she yanked the bed covers off to run towards her bathroom. While throwing up, a pair of hands came up from behind to get her hair out of the way. She was too weak to wonder who it was, and after a few minutes, when she was certain she had emptied her insides, she tried standing up but felt her knees give way. The hands came up to help her again, and she took them, standing up feebly.

'What time is it?' she asked, without looking at him, as he led her back to bed.

'It's about 2 pm.'

'Oh God, no! I missed office?'

'Yes, your assistant called Trisha. She has informed her you will not be available for a week.'

Kavya rested her head in her hands, realising the mess she was in. She had never felt so out of it in twelve years, barring a few instances. Her stomach hurt like her intestines had been cut open. Her bed smelled of puke, and she was not even in her clothes.

'Sorry, I didn't know where your clothes were, so I got you one of my tees,' he said as if reading her mind.

'Was I ... umm ... not wearing any clothes?' she asked, afraid she knew his answer.

'No, you were lying unconscious without clothes, curled up in a ball ... very close to two almost empty vodka bottles. One of them was broken into three huge pieces, and I found you with one of the pieces in your hand.'

As he narrated this using his photographic memory, Kavya began to notice his demeanour. He was cold and distant, almost like she remembered him from the past. He appeared indifferent and withdrawn. What else could she expect from him? She could imagine him coming home after having a good time with Trisha and then finding her like that, lines of disgust creasing his forehead, exactly how he saw her back in Parvatnagar. An unwanted complication.

She was getting angrier every minute. How dare he make her feel unwanted in her own house? Why did he come here? Why wasn't she able to call him out on his selfishness? Why was she losing all control?

'I will get you something to eat. You probably wanna shower and come down. If not, just give me a shout. I will bring your food here.'

He walked away with that emotionless suggestion. There were no questions as to what happened, no curiosity and not an iota of warmth. It seemed like the mask was off, and the real Darsh had resurfaced after all. Getting increasingly uneasy, she reached for her drawer. The tablets were all gone. She searched everywhere but could not find it. She had two from the cabinet downstairs last night, but there were at least ten up here. Where did they go?

Why did life seem to have turned full circle to have brought them back to exactly the same point where they left things? Kavya's mind began playing that clip from the past again. Those memories had tormented her on and off, but today, it felt like actual physical time travel. She was twenty again, and they were in his bungalow. She climbed down the stairs urgently—unchanged, unkempt, barefoot, stuck in that day from her past.

He was in her kitchen with his back to her, pouring hot khichdi out of the cooking pot onto a plate. The smell of fresh tempering filled the house, but Kavya could only smell the moist, stale air from inside his bungalow from twelve years ago. She saw him standing there with her back to her and then looked down at herself. Instead of the T-shirt, she saw herself in the black lingerie she had worn that night. But there was one difference this time. She knew the outcome. She knew how he was going to destroy her when he turned around.

A strange, sharp, high-pitched noise interrupted her thoughts. She saw him turning in a swift moment and then registered that it was coming from her. She couldn't stop it, and it turned into a full-fledged howling in no time. Tears rolled down uncontrollably, and she couldn't lower her volume. He was calling out her name, but his voice was not reaching her. He seemed like he was on the other side of a transparent wall, which blocked his access to her.

She sat down at her tiny kitchen table and cried. To block him from her vision, to block the memories that had crawled back into the present, she kept her head on the table and screamed into the dark safety of her arms. When her crying subsided, it could have been minutes or hours; she looked up gingerly, hoping he was gone. But he was sitting right there, waiting for her.

'Wanna eat?' He pushed the steaming plate towards her.

She ate in perfect silence and waited for the hot ball of anger in her throat to slide down with the food. But it didn't move. It was clamouring to get out today. Her mind was slipping between past and present, and she couldn't stabilise herself. This anger had been with her for more than a decade, searing like lava—mostly dormant in recent times, boiling. And as past and present mingled together today, it seemed that her hate took an actual physical form, independent from her, and decided to step out.

As soon as she had enough food inside to get rid of the queasiness, the plate flew from the table as she pushed it in a rage that was uncharacteristic of her and stood up. He followed the plate with his eyes but didn't react. She made an attempt to wipe the tears off her face and started with the tirade that had been long due.

'You are a sick man, Darsh Purohit. You are not even fit to be a human being. You are sick. You are wrong in your head.' She was loud, and her words came out clear and biting through gritted teeth, curdled rage dripping out of every single one of them. Even as she said these words, it felt strange, like another person had taken over her.

'You don't even realise what you did to me. Otherwise, you wouldn't have had the guts to stroll back into my life as you did.'

She felt her eyes filling up again as she remembered the painstaking preparation she had done for the night. His face blurred as the tears swarmed in, and soon, it seemed like she was talking to herself. He had gone still like a statue, disappearing into the surroundings, present enough to give her the satisfaction of release and absent enough to make her feel uninhibited.

'I was so naive—not even naive, I was an idiot. All that I did was only because I thought I could save you from becoming that character from *The Stranger*, that stupid book you carried around like it was your soul.'

She wiped her eyes again and sniffed, trying to control herself, but the words tripped out of her mouth like an overstuffed closet had just been opened. Her pitch turned lower, almost as if she were talking to herself.

'I was going to be twenty that night and had dared to put myself out there for the first fucking time. For years, I had been burning with feelings for you, but never did I ever impose myself. You kept turning up whenever you wanted and then left as you wished. You treated me like I was disposable.

'It was my fucking birthday! Every birthday after that has been a terrible night, spent alone whimpering. I thought, if sex was important to you, what's the harm? Do you know how much it took out of me to do what I did? Someone who hadn't even the courage to tell you in words what they felt stood there like that.

'How heartless and sick can a guy be to treat someone, like you treated me? You could have kicked me in the face, and it would have hurt the same. First, you made it clear that I was not even worth a meaningless fuck, and then you let that woman in your house even before I left?

'What was my fault? That I loved you despite you being an absolute asshole?'

At the end of her outburst, she thought she was finally able to get a grip on herself. The debilitating anger had left, and all she felt now was sadness.

'I hate you, Darsh. You should leave my house now,' she said quietly in his general direction after a minute of pause. It came out as a well-thought-out decision, and after announcing this, she climbed the stairs towards her room. All the talking had left her immensely exhausted, but she felt lighter. She felt years of weight lifting off her when she reached her room and closed the door.

It was probably for this that fate had brought her face to face with Darsh again—to be able to give him a piece of her mind. His purpose in her life was finally over. She got into her bed and let her mind wander to the night that changed her life forever.

Twenty-Two

After Kavya's dismal board results, she got into one of the local colleges. At home, silence prevailed mostly—a permanent blanket of disappointment wrapped around the Agarwal household. Her mother had started talking about getting her married by the time she finished college, as there wasn't anything else left to do. Kavya escaped this morose air by camping at Riya's on most days. With the recent reinstatement of Darsh in her eyes, after the night when his appearance thwarted her plans of jumping into the river, she started focusing again on how to fix him.

Riya's research from the days she stalked him helped. She told Kavya that as much as Darsh was known around town for sleeping with many women in college, he had never dated anyone, as far as the grapevine went. Kavya could believe that. She knew first-hand that he had nothing but contempt for love, which she needed to fix.

For that, it was essential to find out Darsh's perception of himself. He didn't socialise and spent most of his time alone, trekking in jungles or mountains, reading book after book and having meaningless sex. He had finished college, and no one knew his plans, even though he received a gold medal from the state for securing the highest marks in the current year. A medal that his father received on his behalf because he didn't care. Why did he behave like a complete stranger in the town he was born in?

A stranger. The word struck her like a bolt of lightning, opening up a whole new perspective.*The Stranger*.

The book he always had on him. He carried it everywhere, and she had seen him reading and re-reading it over the years. Why was it so special to him? Did he think of himself as a weird stranger? Could the book act as a gateway to Darsh? She couldn't analyse him, but she could analyse this outsider in the book.

He was surprised when she asked to borrow the book, but readily gave it to her. You might not like it, he said; no one likes it. But Kavya had borrowed it with a purpose. The book presented her with instant answers. It started with the death of the narrator's mother and his inability to feel anything. It turned darker when he murdered someone because he just felt disoriented and uncomfortable at that moment.

Meursault, the narrator and protagonist, responded only to his senses and had no conscience. He was morally bereft and was unable to recognise the consequences of his actions. The book ended with a court finding him guilty of the murder—not because of evidence of the crime, but because of his inability to feel. Darsh was right. She did not like the book, but understood why he liked it. He saw himself in Meursault, finding the same kind of solace with him that people find with friends who don't judge them.

But Kavya knew he was not Meursault. She knew for certain that he could feel things. He had chosen not to feel, but his extraordinary powers of intuition and perception made him acutely aware of all emotions. He was not morally bereft; he refused to sleep with Riya because she was young. He did go and see his mother when she had asked him to. Emotions did bounce off him as things did against a hardened wall, but walls could always be broken down.

Kavya never returned the book, and Darsh didn't ask for it. She obsessed over it and guarded it like a zealot in possession of the Holy Grail. Once she started going to college, her eyes spied a tiny internet café nearby, lined with computers with internet access. She decided to spend time researching this character and the way he had been interpreted over the years. It turned out that the book had been around for a long time and was considered a classic. The author was an existentialist.

That's how Kavya discovered the philosophy of existentialism. At a time when her friends and classmates spent time gossiping over the street food carts around their college gates after class, she would rush to the café, spending hours on Meursault and his existentialism. Albert Camus, its French author, believed that there was no purpose or point to life. People existed, and that's all there was to it. That's why Meursault did not bear any moral responsibility towards his actions. His senses ruled him, and he was free, whether outside jail or inside it.

There was no point to life, Darsh had told her near the dam. He saw his absence of feelings as freedom. But even to reach such a conclusion, someone had to first know that feelings caused pain or hurt. When was he hurt? Did he become what he was because of his mother's violence and his father's indifference? What had attracted him to someone like Meursault? And how could she stop him from turning into this pathetic character who was nothing more than a pack of flesh and bones?

She found the answer in the protagonist's girlfriend. While the man didn't know how to feel love, he most certainly missed spending time with her when he couldn't. Marie accepted him for what he was and asked him for what she wanted without expecting him to understand her feelings. She asked him to take her to the movies, and he did. She asked him to marry her, and he agreed. She understood that the only way Meursault could connect with her was through sex, and she did not judge him for it. She enjoyed being with him, even though he was so different, and that's how they worked.

Kavya spent a lot of time wondering if she could turn into Marie. Darsh didn't like to dabble in feelings, but he had no qualms about sex. She had been battling this conflict for a long time: about having feelings for someone who didn't answer her moral conditioning. She should have abhorred him but she didn't. Was it finally time to give in and accept this side of him? Had she finally found the key to solving the puzzle? Transitioning from a best friend to a one-night stand? That didn't even sound right. How could it be right?

Over the next few weeks, she tried to forget about it, not even telling Riya about this crazy idea. However, the dangling hope of gaining access to Darsh's heart kept luring her back, even if the path was unconventional. The chances of this opening Darsh's heart and life were real. When he slept with people he didn't have to see again, it fit conveniently into the map of his emotionless life. But what if he slept with her, someone he needed, even if erratically? Maybe turning this platonic love into a sexual one would give it a new meaning to Darsh Purohit. Just maybe the small corner he had for her would expand into a legitimate relationship if she broke the boundaries.

This is how a mere, innocent-looking novel changed her course of life. The fate of Meursault triggered Kavya into taking the driver's seat in a relationship she had considered hopeless till now. She didn't have the liberty anymore to leave their future to the rough tides of destiny. She had to pull him from the depths of his unfeeling netherworld.

She chose her birthday to make this transition. She hadn't seen him in a long time, and that fuelled the adrenaline she needed for the step she was going to take. She had done her research. His father was out of town, and it was the weekly off for the house staff. The bungalow would be empty. He had been in his outhouse last night, so there was a good chance he was going to be back tonight, too.

Telling her mom she was going to spend the night at Riya's, she jumped the wall with a large backpack after dinner. Crossing the outhouse that was locked, she moved towards the pristine white bungalow with the stealth of a cat. The sun had long set, and the only lights visible were on the wrap-around balcony, giving the white structure a golden hue. Like a fire was trying to escape from the ground, about to devour the entire building. Ignoring all the ominous signs, she went behind the structure and found the bathroom window on the lower ground floor. She knew it was unused, and half of it always remained open.

Trespassing on someone's property was only the first of many bold, questionable steps she had in mind for tonight. She took a deep breath and jumped through the window, knowing full well there was no going back after this. Her twentieth birthday was going to be a night of transition from Kavya to Marie.

Darsh's bungalow was maintained like a mini palace because of his mother's penchant for regality. The staff maintained the same look even years after she left. Kavya walked around in leisure, taking in the beauty. Surrounded on three sides by the balustraded verandah, the massive living room was dominated by a huge chandelier hanging low right in the middle. Large French windows flanked the walls, and a stream of sunlight filtered through in the daytime to reach the chandelier glass and break into thousand pieces of light fragments scattered across the wooden floor below.

The room gave way to a long corridor leading to other rooms, finally opening up into an open kitchen that was an anomaly—equipped with all modern apparatus in the otherwise old-fashioned set-up. The counter in the middle was big enough to lie down on. She was surprised when a vision of Darsh lying over her on this kitchen top sneaked into her head without warning. She blushed and made her way to his room upstairs. He could come home anytime and would probably stop to fix a meal, as his caretaker was on leave. She had to be ready to surprise him by then.

Twenty-Three

She had been to his room only once when they were kids. Today, it felt like she had come full circle, back there with a mission. She stood in front of the classically styled dresser and put on some make-up. She had purchased a lot of it when starting college, like every other girl, but never really put it on. Somehow, going to college with red lipstick didn't seem right to her, but tonight was different. She wanted to look and feel like a woman.

She aimed to be better than every woman he had been with. She wanted him to say that he would never touch anyone else again. Peering into the mirror intently, she rimmed her eyes with a thick kajal and shaped her brows meticulously. She smoothened her skin with a beige foundation and topped it with red lipstick. Finally, she released the clip that held her hair together, allowing the freshly shampooed tresses to fall to her waist. She was pleased with her reflection. Kavya had left, and Marie was in.

Satisfied with her make-up, she bent over her backpack again and took out a discreet-looking packet. It had taken her three weeks to gather the guts to walk into a fancy lingerie shop and choose one for herself. Before this, she had been content with whatever her mother bought for her. The woman at the store had looked at her suspiciously. It was rare that a young girl would buy her own lingerie. Upon seeing her final choice, she almost went red in the face with the confirmation that this purchase was for some other unholy purpose than modesty.

Kavya changed into the black lacy bra and underwear right in his room, and it felt quite erotic to have done so. All lines had been crossed now except the final one. She had given this everything she had. After putting on the semi-transparent slip that provided a flimsy cover, she gave herself one final look. Her breasts looked fuller, accentuated by the bra. Her thighs were on full display, slender and taut. Tonight, she wasn't something any hot-blooded male could say no to.

Going back downstairs, she worked on the settings in the living room. Two large scented candles came out of her backpack, and she placed them on the ornate stand on the centre table. The chandelier reflected the light that flickered and danced once she lit them up. The setting looked heavenly, and Kavya's heart froze as she heard his bike outside right on time.

She heard the main door open in the distance and sat still in the living room like someone caught in stage fright before a performance. The clock said ten-thirty, one and a half hours to the stroke of midnight. The noise in the kitchen told her he had gone directly to fix his food.

She walked gingerly to the kitchen and saw him there. Busy heating some food on the stove, Darsh stood against the counter with his back to her, his T-shirt discarded carelessly over the back of one of the dining chairs. He stood only in a pair of jeans, his back glistening with sweat from trekking in the jungle, highlighting the taut muscles all over, from naturally toned biceps to the broad shoulders that flexed as he moved around the counter. Never had Kavya been more aware of her sexual desire for him than at that moment. As if to break the spell, something fell off the counter, and Darsh bent down to pick it up.

She tiptoed back to the living room and sat down on the sofa, still like in a picture. He had to come back out and see the lights. Sitting there, bathed in the dancing light, decked up in sexy attire, she was hoping for an allure that would catch him by surprise. He would carry her upstairs and make love to her, breaking his no-intimacy rule and falling for her. Nothing could go wrong.

He must have noticed the flickering lights coming from the living room because she could hear him approaching. He entered, looking confused, and then his gaze rested on her: sitting still as if in a portrait, looking up at him expectantly.

'Kavya? What's going on?' He asked grimly as he put down his stacked dinner plate on a table near the door. There was a slight but clear edge in his voice as he looked around and noticed the changes she had made.

She felt her throat go dry. She had practised her lines a dozen times, but nothing prepared her for how exposed she felt right now under his scrutiny. She stood up then, revealing herself fully as the flame bobbed between them. He waited for a response, all the while burning her with his gaze.

'Darsh, it's my birthday tonight and I have something to ask you.' she said it finally, hoping she sounded cold enough to suit him. Her heart was racing at an alarming speed, confused by the spurt of desire and fear that engulfed her at the same time.

His face was remarkably closed, betraying no reaction as she fumbled with words. She had to hide the gamut of emotions running havoc beneath the surface for it to work. He had to believe all she was offering was cold, indifferent sex and nothing else.

'I want to sleep with you.'

A look of brief discomfort crossed his face before disappearing behind his cold, blank eyes. He walked towards her with measured steps and sat down opposite her.

'Sit.' That's all he said, and Kavya realised she was still standing, almost frozen. She sat down, feeling uneasy at how this was going. As seconds passed by, she could hear her heart hammer inside. She chose not to look at his face and instead stared at the taut muscles on his stomach. She now wished he had a shirt on.

'Listen, Kavya,' he said finally, 'I have had a long day, and there's nothing more I want right now than some mind numbing sex.' He paused after that and then added quite unceremoniously, 'But it can't be you.'

'Why? You think I can't have "mind numbing" sex? I can. I have read ... stuff.' She interjected almost defiantly, edging nearer to him quite unconsciously in her earnestness.

'Listen...' He tried again but she did not want to deal with his refusal. Even though internally she was willing the ground to swallow her, she knew Marie would not give up and go away. She could not let him deny her.

'Or is it because I am not attractive enough for you?' She challenged him and, inspired by a sudden boldness, reached for his hand in an unexpected move and put it on her half-exposed breast.

She held it there, and he looked on wordlessly as if accepting the challenge and letting her watch that she didn't affect him at all. But her nipples had perked up in response to the touch. She let his hand go then, and it fell away from her, not protesting in the least. She felt utterly humiliated, and tears stung her eyes.

'I won't grow wings after we fuck. It's a failed experiment from the start,' he stated emotionlessly and stood back up, indicating the end of conversation. With shock, Kavya saw him approach the centre table and blow out the candles out one by one and throw them in an empty carton nearby with utter indifference.

Mortified that he had guessed her plan, she got up and walked up to face him again, feigning a thick skin she didn't have.

'All I want is to have sex with you, Darsh, that's it,' she said, looking straight at him and adding softly, 'Don't make me beg.'

He perused her from top to bottom this time, not hiding that he was giving her a thorough appraisal. Colour rushed to her face under his gaze as his eyes rested on her breasts and then went lower. For a moment, she thought he was going to agree. She was so wet between her legs she wondered if she had started her period. And then he looked back up at her face and she saw his face harden again.

'No. Get dressed and go home, Kavya,' he said with finality before walking out of the living room, leaving her high and dry.

Alone in the room again, she let it sink in. She had offered herself, half-naked, like an object, and Darsh had rejected her and asked her to get out. Not only had he shut down all hopes of a future, but he had humiliated her without a thought. There was not even friendship left. All he had given her tonight was a searing memory to live with. She felt like she had been branded with a hot iron because that's how much it hurt. She hastily put on her T-shirt and jeans and walked towards the main door, her eyes downcast, but she couldn't resist looking up when she heard voices at the door. She stepped into the shadows and waited, not willing to face them.

A woman had just entered the house, and Darsh was talking to her. She was tall, beautiful and sophisticated. Kavya saw her giving him a flirtatious smile, even as she complained.

'I have been at the door forever, Darsh. I know you like your women to wait, but it's not as exciting outside the bedroom.'

'Make yourself home upstairs. I will get the wine,' he said to her, pointing to the stairs. The moment she went up, Kavya ran out the door past Darsh, unable to breathe, not knowing that the worst night of her life had just begun.

Twenty-Four

She woke up late in the evening after a rare dreamless sleep. The buoyancy that coursed through her veins after finally standing up for herself had stayed. The cross of humiliation that she had been carrying was gone, and she hoped he was, too. After a long, relaxing bath, she put on a yellow flowery dress, even when she had nowhere to go. She carefully rimmed her eyes and painted her lips, combing her tresses and tying them into a neat bun over the head. She admired herself for a minute but wavered a little when she ran her tongue over her lips, and another unpleasant memory flashed in front of her for a split second. Blinding pain passed through her, and her cheeriness flickered like a light bulb about to fuse. She took in a long breath and closed her eyes. She was OK.

The hall was eerily silent downstairs, with only the small kitchen light switched on. She peered at his room, and the door was slightly ajar. Approaching the door, she waited for a sound, but there was none, so she pushed it open only to reveal a neat room empty of all his stuff. The nightstand was devoid of all his books. He had left.

Relief coursed through her as she realised she wouldn't have to face him again. With him gone, she wouldn't have to deal with unpredictable waves of emotions anymore. She could go back to her routine with no room for complications. And now the dull pain that she had been carrying for years, the pain of his cold rejection, seemed to have gone with him. However, as she made her way into the kitchen, right under the ceiling light, a plain envelope addressed to her caught her eye. He had left her a letter.

OK, so he *did* have some things to say.

Kavya sat down on the chair and stared at the envelope. Her name had been neatly scribbled in the centre with black ink. She picked it up finally and tore it open. Her hand shook slightly as she unfolded a single sheet of paper covered in his familiar handwriting.

Kavya,

This apology is twelve years late and probably irrelevant, but I want you to know I am sorry.

I was selfish and self-centred, insensitive and cold, utterly incapable of basic empathy. But I was also terrified.

As a little boy, I often ran towards my parents' room after a nightmare. I wanted nothing more than to be hugged by my mother for comfort. But the door stayed locked. No amount of need would make her open the door. I think while growing up, you became that door for me: I wanted it to be there, but I never wanted to need it to open again … because what if it didn't? I was a selfish prick; I didn't want you to stop being there for me even when I had nothing to give you. That's probably why I kept my distance. I thought if I let you in, you would realise how worthless I was, and leave.

It took me years of therapy and a lot of hard work to figure myself out. I registered long ago that my behaviour was extremely toxic and might have hurt you way more than I ever imagined. I thought about finding you multiple times but always stopped short, wondering if it was right to disrupt your life when you might have buried the past a long ago. In short, I kept making excuses to myself so that I didn't have to own up to anything.

But coming here, I saw you haven't buried anything. You were seething silently, but we could never really talk about it until today. It took you a full-blown mental breakdown to release your anger, which was probably good. I know you would feel good about it for some time, and I wish I could tell you that all your problems are solved, but that would be lying.

I would be lying if I told you I have forgotten the panic attack you had that night in the forest or that I have not wondered if there's something else you want desperately to forget but instead have been internalising it. You are not OK, Kavya. You need help. And you don't need the drugs. You need therapy.

I also realised yesterday that I was your trigger. It makes me sad that no matter how badly I want to help you with your pain, I am the one who is causing it.

It's necessary to find a psychotherapist to help you navigate out of the maze of feelings inside you. I fully acknowledge and appreciate the pain I have caused you, but there's something more hurting you than what happened with us. Unless you work through everything that's hurt you with a professional, things will keep haunting you. I have made you a list of the best counsellors in the city, picking only those who don't know me. I have also taken the liberty of asking Trisha to stay with you for some time. I know you think it's unnecessary and you are feeling just fine, but the anxiety and the attacks creep up most unexpectedly. After what happened on Monday evening, it's not a good idea to stay alone for the time being.

I would like to end this letter by telling you something that you have known all along, but it's important that I admit it.

That night was not your fault; it was mine.

You were brave. You reached out, and I know now that it would have taken a lot of courage to place yourself in a vulnerable position like that. But back then, I couldn't see how my reaction affected you. I couldn't appreciate how big a deal it was for you. When I said no, I was not thinking about how it would make you feel. It was all about me.

But even when I was so damaged, I knew you were a lot worth more than 'a meaningless fuck'. I couldn't risk it. My fear of losing your unconditional love made me stay away, physically and emotionally. My selfishness caused you so much pain, and any amount of apology won't fix it, but please know that I have been sorry for who I was every single day for a very long time.

Love,

Darsh

A tear slid down her cheek unnoticed and blotted the ink where he had written his name. Her happiness dissipated instantly, just like he had predicted in the letter. The letter should have made her happier, as it contained an apology she had dreamt of for many years. Yet, she felt empty and lonely. She sat on the chair for a long time; the will to move even an inch had left her. She could sit still for years, and it wouldn't change a thing in her world. She could die, her corpse rotting in this chair, yet nothing would change in her world. Hopelessness engulfed her like she was in a bottomless pit. She wanted to hit the ground, but there was no ground.

And then someone pressed the doorbell. She ignored it as she couldn't move. But it kept ringing, and after a while, her phone started buzzing, too. Finally, drawing from the meagre reserve of strength she was left with, she walked to the door with heavy, reluctant steps. As informed by Darsh in his letter, Trisha had arrived with a bag that made it evident that she was going to stay. Kavya couldn't even find the will to argue and just let her in wordlessly.

'Oh my god, Kavya, you look so good. But what's with the tears? And why did you take so long to open the door?'

Trisha's chatter annoyed her, and she just went and slid into her sofa, ignoring her. She had no idea how much Darsh had told her, and she didn't find it in herself to even ask. She closed her eyes to withdraw from everything around her.

'Kavya, Kavya,' Trisha's voice finally managed to pierce through the dark alleys her mind had been venturing into. She opened her eyes, left with no other option but to engage with her.

'Here, I made you this mug of green tea.' Trisha thrust it in her hand and sat cross-legged on the sofa right beside her. Did her bangles jingle more than usual, or was it Kavya's high-strung nerves that magnified every noise? Trying her best to cover up her irritation, she sat up to attempt a conversation.

'Trisha, what did Darsh tell you? Why did he send you packing here?'

'He told me you are going through a low phase, and he needs to move out, so someone should keep you company. But why are you giving him credit for me being here? I have been there for you long before he even arrived on the scene, OK?'

Kavya nodded, remembering the way they first met. Since then, Trisha had been guarding Kavya with impressive zeal and did not even know the whole story.

'I am feeling low, yes, and I need a complete break from everything.'

'Not from me, no. I have already told my boss I will be working from home for at least a week. I am not leaving your side at all.'

'I will go to bed now. I am feeling exhausted. You make yourself at home and put your stuff in that room. Let's talk tomorrow.'

'No, what about dinner? Let me order some delicious Chinese, and we can watch a movie.'

The remarkable thing about Trisha was that she had no qualms about imposing, and as annoying as it seemed to Kavya, given the present situation, her non-confrontational personality didn't allow her to refuse again. That's how Trisha almost always got her way with her, anyway, whether it was a night out at a pub in the middle of the week or a pathetic movie that only she wanted to watch.

She sank back into her sofa and stared at Trisha flipping channels, realising how uninteresting the world had suddenly become. She couldn't care less about anything. Once the food arrived, she ate it mechanically, with no sense of hunger or taste.

'So, you went out with him, right? You are seeing him now?' she finally asked, scooping up the rubbery fried rice from her box.

Trisha's face clouded slightly as she paused the movie and turned to face her.

'No, I am not. And, Kavya, he did meet me, but it was not a date as I had imagined. He said he was meeting me only to clear the air, OK?'

'Why are you explaining this to me? I already told you it doesn't matter to me.'

'It matters. You slipped into this phase right after I told you that we were probably going to see each other. You can't ignore that.'

Kavya felt flustered at the straight talk. She got up to go to her room.

'It's not that simple,' she told her, abandoning any attempt to hide how upset she was and turning towards the steps to go to her room. Halfway up the stairs, when she had put enough distance between herself and her friend, she asked the question that was killing her.

'You know where he went?'

Trisha did not answer, but the little grimace on her face that appeared was enough to tell her that she knew.

'Tell me then.'

'How does it matter, Kavya?'

'I would like to know.'

'He said he was going back ... to the US.'

Sleep came in disturbed waves. She woke up several times, and the awareness that Darsh had left rushed back to her. She likened it to his abrupt departure from Parvatnagar, even though this time, it was she who told him to leave. Ignoring that logic, her mind labelled him as the one who abandoned her yet again and conjured anger for him from unknown places.

Twenty-Five

Trisha made herself at home in the downstairs room, which had been occupied by Darsh just twenty-four hours ago. She went into the bathroom to wash her face and was mildly disturbed at how his aftershave still hung in the air. On their dismal date, he had revealed some things that she was still reeling from. That was the reason she was surprised to have received a call from him on the same night they had decided not to keep in touch. When she answered, his voice betrayed further stress. He wanted to know if Kavya had demonstrated any unhealthy drinking behaviour in the past. She told him she was the one who drank more than her share, while Kavya always exercised control. He then asked her if she habitually took unplanned leaves from the office or arrived late. Trisha couldn't think of a single such instance.

'Something has triggered her then.' His voice was so low it seemed like he was talking to himself.

'Is she OK? Should I come over?'

'She will be fine but inform someone at work that she might not be available for a few days. She has had a breakdown and might need some time off.'

'But why? All of a sudden?'

'I will be in touch. She might need you,' he had said before hanging up.

He had called her the following evening, asking her if she could stay with Kavya, and she had agreed instantly. She felt a nagging guilt as she remembered her last text had gone unanswered, which was unusual. Was it her text that caused her such pain? She had been blind to all the signs. She should not have come between them.

Since that evening, Trisha had not been in the best of spirits. The things he told her made her sad. She lay on her bed, staring at the ceiling when sounds of loud sobbing came from upstairs. It made her sit up nervously. What had happened now? After a minute's hesitation, she got up and climbed the stairs, unable to stop herself.

The door was half ajar, and she pushed it open wider. Kavya was sitting on her bed, her head between her knees and her arms folded around them. Loud sobs jerked her body, and she seemed to have given up on any restraint. Trisha stepped inside and reached instinctively to touch her arm, but Kavya recoiled instantly and raised her tear-stained face towards her.

'What's wrong?' Trisha asked, a little nervous about rubbing her the wrong way again.

'I don't know. I just can't stop crying. I feel so sad, and I don't even know why. I feel like it's never going to be OK.'

There was no immediate response Trisha could think of.

'It's all his fault. Why did he waltz in here knowing what he had done?'

'What had he done?' she hesitantly asked, but Kavya ignored it and burrowed her head in her arms again.

Trisha just sat there, waiting for her to calm down. After a few minutes of watching her suffer like that, unable to touch or hold her, she threw all caution to the wind and spoke her mind.

'You know, Kavya, have you given a thought to seeing a therapist or something?'

'Why would I need a therapist? Why are you speaking his language? He is an impostor; nothing he says is real.' Her response was muffled, as she did not even raise her head this time.

'It's not about him, and you need to talk. You need to talk to someone who knows how to help you deal with all this stuff. A person who has the experience and, most importantly, a license.'

'I am dealing just fine.'

'I can do the work for you, Kavya. I can find out who to contact. I will drive you, and I will sit with you. Just try it once and then decide.'

Kavya felt sorry for Trisha, who had been dragged into her hell without any fault. Her earnestness was difficult to ignore, and it would have been plain cruel to brush her off. She attempted feebly to pull herself together and looked up again.

'You don't have to do this. It's my mess.'

'You feel like my mess,' Trisha replied instantly, tearing up a little.

Kavya sighed, feeling more contrite than ever at Trisha's genuine distress. Perhaps she owed her a better response.

'I already have a list. I will make an appointment if you say so. But all I am promising is one session.'

'Deal.' Trisha gave her a broad smile, and some of the warmth reached Kavya's cold and tired heart. She smiled a weak smile of gratitude before they said good night.

Kavya chose a random name from Darsh's letter and fixed an appointment for the next day. 'You don't need drugs; you need therapy,' he had written in the letter. It meant he knew she wasn't crazy in medical terms; no one was going to give her electric shocks or sedate her. Random research on the net had revealed that therapists were not authorised to provide any medications; only psychiatrists could do that. Armed with this knowledge, she felt comparatively safer booking a therapist. Trisha offered to drive again, as Kavya was in jitters. Kavya acknowledged how grateful she felt now that she was not alone, even though she had hated the idea of her being around initially.

As Trisha waited in the lobby, Kavya made her acquaintance with her psychotherapist. Ms Dahlia Reddy looked well into her fifties and wore glasses on the tip of her nose. Her hair was completely white, cropped very short. Dressed in a simple white kurta, she had a gravity about her, coupled with a soft and compassionate face. The room was unremarkable, with two dining-style chairs and a discreet couch in the corner. A small, low table was placed opposite the chairs with a stack of tissue papers and a jug of water. The walls were bare except for a large analogue clock mounted high on the wall. The room looked like a capsule, sealed away from the world.

Dahlia started by asking her to feel comfortable and safe, giving her the references of some organisations that she belonged to, and aiming to assure Kavya that anything she discussed here would be confidential.

'Now, let's start with your current feelings. What brings you here?'

'Well, it's nothing much. I realise it was unnecessary,' said Kavya, getting cold feet.

Dahlia nodded and picked up a small notebook from her side table.

'OK, but since you are here for the next forty-five minutes, we might as well talk about it, don't you think? Have you been feeling low?'

'I suppose,' Kavya said cautiously.

'And what made you decide to seek help? Was there an immediate instance that pushed you to take this first step? Because I know how difficult it is to decide whether you want to handle things alone or see a therapist.'

The therapist was right. The next one hour had already been paid for, and here was a listener who was under oath not to judge or tell anyone.

'It's been a few days. I drank too much with a combination of some pills. Things really went overboard after years, and I just sort of don't trust myself not to repeat that behaviour.'

'You say after years, so you have found yourself … in this situation before?' Dahlia remarked astutely.

'Well, I had a phase like that in college, and it was immediately after Darsh left. But it was twelve years ago.'

Dahlia almost leapt at the inadvertent mention of his name.

'Tell me about Darsh.'

Twenty-Six

It eventually took three more sessions for Kavya to talk about Darsh. The forty-five minutes the therapist offered in each of these sessions were spent mostly on generic things, followed by silence whenever either of them mentioned his name.

She wrestled with the idea of cancelling her upcoming sessions more than once, reminding herself that they somehow made her feel better, even if she couldn't bring herself to talk about Darsh. At first, she wanted to convince Dahlia that he had nothing to do with her problems, but it quickly became clear that unless she spoke about him openly, therapy wouldn't progress. And it didn't hurt that she had begun to like Dahlia Reddy. Her office had started to feel like an actual safe space.

So, with a previously untapped determination – coupled with Trisha's relentless insistence – she made a few conscious decisions to commit to long-term therapy. She applied for a six-month sabbatical from work, choosing to focus on her mental health, to fix herself for good. She also cleared the house of all alcohol and medication, and asked Trisha not to allow her any self-pity on her weaker days.

With this kind of homework and resolve, she drove to Dahlia Reddy's office for her fourth session, reminding herself repeatedly that she was ready to release some of the pain she had carried within her for so many years.

Once she allowed herself to breach the topic, it was like the floodgates had opened. She spoke for nearly half an hour and unloaded all of her history and the feelings she'd carried since Darsh's reappearance. Egged on by Dahlia's quiet nods and her intent gaze, she went into detail about her twentieth birthday at his bungalow, eager to prove that it was he who had started it all. She blamed him outright for shattering her self-esteem for life. She talked about her panic attacks resurfacing, and how she had suffered a mammoth one in the forest.

However, when she reached the part about the letter he had left her, Dahlia stopped writing in her diary and looked up.

'You believe him? The reasons he gave you for rejecting you that night?' she asked pointedly.

Kavya paused, scouring her mind for an honest answer.

'Yes,' she heard herself say slowly. 'I've been thinking about it a lot. Why would a guy who openly admitted to sleeping around indiscriminately say no to someone offering him exactly that? I did everything possible to get him to agree, but he didn't. Maybe he was afraid...'

She paused again, then gave words to the thought that had been haunting her ever since she read the letter.

'He was afraid that I would stop being there for him if he slept with me.'

'So, it's a very likely possibility that he didn't reject you at all, but tried to keep you close by refusing to sleep with you?' Dahlia said gently.

'Yes. It makes sense, doesn't it?'

'If you ask me, yes.'

'Then why am I not feeling better? I was doing just fine before he came back into my life and brought all this mess with him.'

'Well, the fact that his return caused you to slip back into old patterns might be an indication that you weren't actually fine before he arrived?'

'But it was OK. I'd get up, follow my routine, go about life without crying or falling apart like this. Yes, the hurt was there – like a stab wound that hadn't healed – but it didn't sear anymore, you know what I mean?'

'Yes, I see what you mean. You know, anger is a great defence mechanism. And anger that's gone cold can act like a painkiller. Do you see why? When the person isn't around to defend themselves, your belief about them stays unchallenged. But suppose – as in your case – the person returns, apologises and gives you a plausible reason for what they did: where does that leave you?'

Kavya stood up and paced the room. She felt a surge of restlessness. She had to hold on to the hate somehow, but it had been leaving her in a steady trickle since her outburst and the letter.

'It leaves me terrified, actually. I don't know what to feel anymore. I am not that angry, but I want to be. It's frustrating to realise he is not cold and heartless. I want to hate him, but his recent behaviour and his letter do not permit me to. I think I am terrified of not being angry,' Kavya offered, surprised by how easy it was to figure it out when her thoughts were being led in the right direction. She sat back on her chair resignedly but, weirdly, felt better.

But all that relief evaporated when Dahlia asked her next question.

'It seems natural to me that you feel terrified, faced as you are with a shift in your feelings after years. Being aware of how you feel is important.

'Let's talk more about that night, if that is OK with you. What happened next? I mean, after you left his house. You must have been feeling terrible.'

Kavya closed up instantly. Her body became taut, and she could feel faint goosebumps on her exposed arms. The room became uncomfortably cold.

'Do you have the AC on by any chance? I am cold,' she informed Dahlia, managing not to look her in the face.

Dahlia suggested she wear her jacket as the AC was already switched off, all the while watching her carefully. Kavya wore her jacket in silence.

'So, how did you react when you left his house? Were you able to sleep?'

She could not talk about what happened next. It was unnecessary and did not need to be discussed. The chills she felt that night as she stormed out of his house into the cold had come back to assail her. She was cold and uncomfortable. She wanted to stand up, make an excuse and leave the room at that moment, but it felt like something was weighing her down, and she could not move. Dahlia decided to speak then, and what she said reassured Kavya to a certain extent, and she felt her heart slowing down.

'It's totally OK if you don't want to talk about it, Kavya. You will do it when you want to. Here, we talk about things you want to.'

And right then, as if on cue, the clock struck, indicating that her time was over. The therapist closed her notebook quietly and removed her glasses.

'I find it interesting, though, that you mentioned his presence helped you in fighting a panic attack you had in the forest. There could be more to these attacks than just him. Perhaps we will talk more about your childhood next, to explore the root of these attacks?'

The root of these attacks.

Kavya thought about it all the way home as Trisha drove quietly after being assured that another session was already booked. She had locked the rest of her birthday night in the most inaccessible corner of her brain. What had happened after she left his house could not be the real reason for her misery. It was nothing, after all. She had overreacted as she was too young, allowing the experience to debilitate her for an entire year. Therefore, once she was able to get back up on her feet, she thought she had erased the memory permanently.

However, Dahlia Reddy's casual inference that the root of her misery lay elsewhere was proof enough that it was still imprinted all over her. It was a reminder that, at some point, everything that happened after she left his house had to come to the surface, even if it meant unlocking the secret chambers of her brain. The mere thought made her palms sweaty, and her heart quickened a notch.

Twenty-Seven

'You can take your time, Kavya. There's no hurry,' Dahlia told her when she noticed her stress. 'You have already made some good progress in my opinion.'

'You think? Well, I do feel I have got some kind of closure with Darsh, for all it's worth.'

'That's good. And I agree. You seem to have progressed on resolving your feelings about your last encounter with him.'

'Yes, his letter helped. You know what all this means, Dahlia? In some weird way, even though I feel more terrible than before, it is sort of progress,' Kavya said uncertainly.

'Oh yes, you are here, aren't you?' Dahlia smiled in reply. 'Now, do you feel like talking about these panic attacks? You talked about one in the woods when you were with him.'

Kavya prepared to speak, even though waves of unpleasantness engulfed her at the thought of discussing those. Her voice came out small and wary.

'They started sometime after that night and were very frequent for a year or so. But over the years, I learnt to manage them, and they grew less frequent with time.'

'How did you manage them?'

'Most times with medication and sometimes with breathing exercises ... but they were almost gone until he arrived here.'

Dahlia nodded. 'Yes, naturally, he brought the past with him. Any other changes happened to you after that night, Kavya?'

Kavya hesitated and stayed silent, yet Dahlia continued waiting, looking at her intently over her glasses.

'I cannot say for sure if it started right after that night, but I noticed that I developed an aversion to touch,' she said finally.

Dahlia scribbled a little longer into the notebook after this revelation and then looked up at her. 'Why do you think that happened?'

'I don't know. I think I just do not want to be touched. It could very well be a conscious decision. It's not like I feel my life is any less.'

Dahlia remained silent, and Kavya realised she was expecting her to go on.

'I remember feeling hot for him, you know. I remember that physical yearning in my body, but it all just dried up after that night. I cannot even stand the thought of sex. It disgusts me, the idea of exposing myself that way to anyone.'

'It disgusts you, or you fear it?'

Kavya shrugged. 'Physical gestures of affection horrify me. Most of the time, I just excuse myself after I am subjected to a situation like that, quite ably managing my reactions. But there are times I look at anyone's hands about to touch me, and I feel like puking. Sometimes, the reaction I feel is unreasonably strong, like shortness of breath … sometimes I freeze … I get even claustrophobic if someone comes close, even unintentionally.'

She saw Dahlia shift at that confession. Her eyes bored into hers as she spoke again.

'Would you mind if we went back to that night again? It's important if we want to really explore the cause of your aversion. Is that OK?'

Kavya nodded, and Dahlia turned to a previous page in her notebook.

'So, I know you left his house rather upset. How did you handle your feelings once you were on your own? Can you take me through to the next part of the night?'

Kavya felt her legs turn into jelly as she swallowed hard. She had put layers of haphazard bandages over that patch of her memory, and now she was being asked to uncover the ugly wound and look right at it.

Dahlia Reddy flipped back a few pages in her diary, underlined something and looked back at Kavya with a serious expression.

'It's not the first time you have ignored this question, Kavya. If there is something you are running away from, there's a strong chance that talking about it could give us some solutions…'

Kavya just stared at the clock on the wall behind Dahlia. One half of her wanted the clock to strike again, and the other half wanted to spill her guts out. It dawned on her that she wanted to talk about it to Dahlia, especially because she did not label this touch situation a mental condition right away, like that therapist in college.

Dahlia leaned back into her chair, and her eyes softened with understanding as she saw Kavya's dilemma on her face. She offered her a way out.

'There are many ways to express it, Kavya, even if you don't want to talk about it. If I give you a paper, can you write it down for me?'

Kavya felt flustered as she nodded. Her palms were sweaty again, and she felt a little constricted around her neck. Her hands trembled as she put the pen against the blank paper. What had happened to her? Could she finally acknowledge it through the word that was clamouring to come out on the paper? Slowly, deliberately, she spelt it out.

'A-S-S-A-U-L-T'

She was about to hand the paper back, but she felt a little emboldened now as the first word was out. Below the word, she labelled it for what it was.

'S-E-X-U-A-L'

Dahlia took the piece of paper and read it expressionlessly. Nothing in her demeanour changed, and Kavya felt a huge relief. With relief came the tears. Dahlia handed her the tissues, and she wiped her face quietly.

'Have you ever talked about it to anyone? A friend or family?'

'My mother and a friend back home know, but I have never talked about it. They just knew. Because of ... you know my situation at that time...'

'I see. You feel prepared to talk about it?'

'I don't remember a lot. It's like a hazy memory, and I have worked hard to forget about it.'

'That makes sense, but memories, if they have been internalised, need to be processed for them to lose their hold over you. But as I said, it's your call, and you decide the pace.

'However, I would like you to do an exercise for me before we meet again. Do you have anyone in your life right now who is close, and you trust them?'

Kavya had only one person in her life like that, and she nodded, thinking of Trisha at home.

'And I am assuming you have trouble being held or touched by her as well?'

'Yes. Except for Darsh, I feel the same way about everyone. It felt normal with him. In fact, it was only when I hugged him after the panic attack in the forest that I realised I hadn't been in a physical embrace forever … and it did feel … good.'

The therapist made a few notes about it but did not comment on her confession about Darsh.

'So, over the next few days, I would like you to make a conscious effort to touch Trisha, like hold her hands or even hug her, if you think you can. Time it. If you can only do it for a second, that's all right too. But start by exposing yourself a little to this fear.'

The clock struck and announced that her fifty minutes were over, and Kavya stood up, feeling unsure. As she collected her jacket, she threw a last question at Dahlia.

'So you don't think I have a medical condition or something? Is there a chance it fixes itself?'

'Well, I don't know, but you just told me you already felt normal … even nice, after the human warmth you received at the forest ... so I would say we have no reasons not to be optimistic.'

When Kavya left the building and got into her car, she caught herself smiling a little. Take that, she muttered to the therapist back in college who had made her feel she was a mental patient. She could get past this. She drove back with a newfound confidence that she could be normal again.

Twenty-Eight

Kavya could not sleep the following night as the intense fear of her nightmares returned with a vengeance. She reached for her meds but found none. At around three, she went downstairs, wondering if moving around her house would distract her. She found Trisha asleep on her couch with the TV on. She walked over to the couch and watched her, acknowledging again how her presence made a difference. She had convinced herself that she liked being alone and did not like being touched, but this extremely unsettling phase and her therapy had revealed that her past was still dictating her reactions. Once she understood that, she desperately wanted to break free.

She sat quietly on the couch, ensuring her movement did not disturb Trisha. The duvet and Trisha's body transferred a small amount of warmth to her, giving her a reprieve from the nightmarish memories. She looked at Trisha's hand, resting on her side, limp and lifeless. That girl had attempted numerous times to hold her and hug her, always receiving an icy response.

Kavya looked hard at the still hand and wondered what made her so wary. Why was it that she felt an instant need to recoil or move away from touch, even as benign as Trisha's? She forced herself to reach out for it, and as their skin came in contact, she felt an uneasiness in her stomach pit. She did not let it go, though, asking herself, daring herself to feel the disgust, hoping it would give her an answer.

The bile steadily rose to her throat as she dared and entwined her fingers into Trisha's hand. It sent her straight to the dark night in the forest when two rough hands had pressed hers into the ground, hurting her. The hands were coarse and big and had landed on her mouth to suffocate her as she tried to scream.

Suddenly, Trisha's hands turned into the hands of her nightmares, bigger, rougher, coarser. She let them go and ran to the bathroom just in time to throw up as vivid memories came rushing back to her in incessant waves. Too tired to resist, she opened the locked doors inside her head and let herself go back fully to that night, which changed her life.

* * *

She walked in a frenzy, away from Darsh's house and hers too, eager to put distance between herself and the humiliation. It was past midnight and officially her birthday, but her whole world had come crashing down. She continued to put one foot in front of the other as her brain clouded with more and more unpleasant thoughts. The cold, sharp wind cut through her skin relentlessly. The physical hurt was keeping her distracted from the mental pain. It was like her body was racing against her mind. She couldn't afford to stop or even look where she was going.

The residential part of the town was soon behind her. It was the farthest she had come without her bicycle, and she stepped away from the roads into the woods. The trail became rougher, the trees taller and darker, but unaware of anything around her, she kept walking like a maniac. And then suddenly, out of nowhere, someone grabbed her from behind. One hand went over her mouth and the other was pushing her down on the forest floor. Her first reaction was frozen panic, making it easier for her attacker to get her down as no resistance was offered. When she started fighting, it was too late. He was over her, pinning her to the ground securely, one hand still over her mouth.

She tried to scream, but he was too strong for her to move. He was panting like a dog and stank of alcohol and sweat. She fought harder when his hands roved under her T-shirt but to no avail. He had her pinned and could do anything with her. She started kicking vigorously, and she must have hurt him somewhere because he flinched and swore before losing his grip on her. She sprang up in that moment and ran for her life. But in no time, he caught up with her, and this time, cold steel touched the back of her neck as he grabbed her.

'If you don't want to get killed, you will stop fighting.' The voice was dripping with cold anger and frustration, and Kavya believed him. She started sobbing in fear as he led her to a denser patch and threw her on the floor. It was dark, but his weapon glinted as he lowered himself down again. Kavya braced herself for whatever was to come. Placing his knife close by, he pressed both her hands against the ground and took her mouth in his by force. A shot of excruciating pain blazed through her, even as his mouth tried to invade her tightly sealed lips.

Angry at her resistance, he raised himself, and the next thing Kavya saw was his hand coming down on her face. He slapped her hard across the face a few times, giving her an instant bloody upper lip. Then his hands went under her T-shirt, and he mauled her like a wild animal ravaging its prey. He tried slipping his hand in her jeans but then decided he had played around enough. With the knife at her throat, he unzipped himself, and Kavya averted her gaze in acute fear to avoid screaming again. The next moment, she felt something hard pressing against her as he fumbled with her zip.

As fear gripped her, she thought she was going to pass out with the shock of what was about to befall her. And then something strange happened. She started screaming involuntarily. The fear of being stabbed was very much there, but her body was acting without her brain's consent. He seemed unprepared for this and quickly reached to put his hand on her mouth while trying to get hold of the knife that had fallen to the side with his other hand. Kavya kicked him again, and he swore.

Her screams didn't stop, and then suddenly, the siren of what seemed like a police vehicle pierced through the night. The vehicle was racing along the adjacent road to the forest, and Kavya hoped to God they had heard her screaming and were responding. The attacker didn't wait to find out. He grabbed the knife and disappeared deeper into the forest. Kavya lay there for a minute, unable to comprehend that she had been saved. She felt she was still pinned to the ground, and sweat began to gather at the back of her head. As the siren sound faded, her survival instinct overpowered her post-traumatic state of suspension, and she got up and started running back towards the road.

On the night she had wanted to sleep with Darsh, she was almost raped by a drunk faceless man who left her hurting in the middle of the forest.

She ran to Riya's house as she could not bear to face her mother. The night was spent in a daze as the reality of what happened started settling in. Riya, shocked by her state when she arrived and then piecing together the incoherent bits that came out of Kavya's mouth, did not know how to comfort her. When Kavya couldn't sleep, Riya got her some vodka. Kavya drank till her eyes closed of their own accord, and her consciousness slipped into oblivion.

She was able to hide it from her mother for over a month by finding excuses to stay at Riya's most nights. These nights were spent training her mind to deny what happened to her because she felt ashamed of it. She kept repeating that she hadn't been raped and it was just a skirmish that was forgettable. Riya agreed to whatever made her friend feel better. Her only other solace was the unlimited drinking possible at Riya's place because she often woke up screaming if she fell asleep sober.

In the back of her mind, she knew she was sinking fast. She was cutting classes, and it was just a matter of time before her parents found out. Then Riya gave her another piece of news that sucked the rest of her life out of her. Darsh had left town forever, moving to a US medical school. He had not attempted to get in touch at all after that night, and the bitter end to their story made Kavya feel even more lost. That night, after another round of binge drinking, Kavya tried what Riya had tried before in the same house. She found a razor blade in the spare bathroom and would have sunk it into her skin if not for Riya's timely intervention. Riya then suggested she should tell her parents, as things were getting out of hand. And she hinted strongly that she would not encourage any more overnight stays at her place.

Once Kavya started spending more nights at home, it was impossible to hide her state. The screaming in the middle of the night brought her mother into her bedroom a few nights later. She saw her drenched in sweat, with wide, afraid eyes, fighting back in the middle of a nightmare and instantly knew. Kavya never discussed what happened in detail, except that she was saved, and miraculously never pressured to talk about it.

Her mother became her pillar of strength after that night, something she had never expected. Getting professional help was out of the question in Parvatnagar, but having your mother as an ally was the next best thing. Since her father worked night shifts, her mother arranged for Kavya to sleep in their bedroom for a long time. Every time she would wake up screaming, her mother was there, hugging her till she was breathing normally again. When she had phases where she blamed herself, she was there to tell her it was not her fault. When she dropped a year, it was her mother who convinced her father that it was needed. She even pulled a contact in a local medical store and got her pills without a prescription when the hugs were not enough.

Her friends assumed she was grieving because Darsh left, and that's why she dropped a year, a misconception that her mother was happy to support for once. After a year of suffering significant post-traumatic stress, Kavya eventually got better. She learnt to handle her trauma, barring occasional episodes. She resumed college, and life, for the most part, seemed to have got back on track.

When she had first heard that Darsh left for the US to study medicine in a prestigious school, it made her hate him more, but with him out of reach, she channelled all her pain into ambition. She did not want the town to look at her as the poor girlfriend who was ditched. With the new feeling of gratitude coursing through her for her mother, she decided to give her what she had always wanted: a successful daughter she could boast about. She joined a local MBA coaching institute and started leveraging the internet to procure resources to study.

After three long years of hard work, when Kavya finally scored enough to be selected in one of the top five business schools, she thought she had won. For once, she found herself agreeing with her parents' hypothesis. Maybe it was Darsh who had been pulling her down, because with him out of the picture, she was putting herself first and going places. Eventually, she buried the traumatic details of her assault underneath the pain of unrequited love and rejection, blaming Darsh for everything.

She felt strong enough to take on the world when she left home. But she didn't know that the trauma she had suffered was too deep to have disappeared without a trace. She had never talked about it with anyone. All she had done was suppress it. Even when she told Riya about it, she hid all the details. The dense forests on the campus sent a chill down her spine after sunset. She would find herself drenched in sweat in the middle of a class. She found it extremely difficult to participate in any stage event and had built tall walls around herself without realising it.

The first time she found out that she was averse to touch was when a guy in her class tried to hold hands while dropping her to her room after dinner. She jerked her hand away immediately and felt her hair rise all over her body. Feeling hot all over, she thought she would faint in reaction to a slight attempt at intimacy from the unsuspecting classmate.

When she came back to her room, a turbulent night followed, where all the memories of being touched with force came alive. She could smell the sweat and the taste of blood in her mouth as she tried to bite the strange hand that had clamped her mouth shut. When she tried to sleep, she saw it happening all over again in her nightmare. The invading hand that just wouldn't stop. She could hear the sound of the dry leaves being crunched and the strange hard mass that kept rubbing against her pants. After months, she had to pop a pill to calm herself down. From that day onwards, Kavya steered clear of anyone who showed even the slightest romantic interest in her.

Twenty-Nine

After twelve years of denying the seriousness of the assault, this process finally forced Kavya to acknowledge it. Holding Trisha's hand and forcing herself to go through the consequences caused a major shift. She had to accept that a big chunk of her present problems came from that night and she needed to talk about it. So, she bravely prepared herself to face Dahlia's questions in the next session.

Dahlia looked at her with an expression of careful compassion.

'Do you want to talk about it today?'

'Yes.'

She could not bring herself to speak after that. A pregnant silence hung in the air as minutes passed, with Dahlia looking at her expectantly. Finally, her therapist broke the silence.

'That's an intensely traumatic event to have happened to anyone, more so to a twenty-year-old. I am sure it makes you devastated to think about it. There is no rush. Let's try another approach. I will ask you a few questions. You can answer if you want to. That sounds OK?'

Kavya nodded.

'Was it after you left Darsh's house? On the same night?'

'Yes.'

'Was it someone you knew?'

'No.'

Dahlia noted her responses in between, managing to keep giving her a feeling of safe haven with her encouraging nods and no-rush approach.

'So where did it happen, Kavya?'

'In the forest. I … I did not go back to my place … I am fucking stupid … I walked right … into it…'

That was all she could manage, with gritted teeth and a lifetime of regret, before the tears descended on her, and she abandoned all efforts to stay in control. Dahlia handed her the tissues and gave her the space to get a grip.

After what seemed like an eternity, when her sobs seemed quieter, Dahlia's voice came out soothing yet firm.

'So you feel guilty. While that is natural, here's something to think about: you did not know what was going to happen. You were nineteen. You were under emotional stress. You could have done nothing to prevent it except develop a supernatural ability to foresee things.'

'I could have gone back to my house.'

'But you did not… because you did not know. You had no way of knowing, Kavya.'

'And what about Darsh? Darsh could have prevented it all from happening. He could have. It was his fault I was in that jungle.'

Dahlia leaned back on her chair, picking up her pen and getting back to her notebook.

'So you blame yourself and Darsh.'

'He was the reason I was so upset—at least you accept that, right?' Kavya was getting upset at Dahlia's absence of support.

'What I accept and think is not important. What you feel is.'

'I feel he could have done things differently.'

'Maybe. If you knew, you would have gone back to your house and not into the forest. If he knew, he probably would have ensured that you go to your room and nowhere else. A million things could have been done differently. But the fact is, you both had no idea that something like that was going to happen.'

The room became silent after that, as Kavya was given some time to process this perspective.

'Kavya,' Dahlia spoke again, 'I think what will empower you today is if you accept your past. What happened that night was not in your control and not in Darsh's control. But how you deal with this "open wound" now is. This attitude of acceptance, and then a gradual process of dissociating with the "responsibility" you feel for the assault, might ensure you move forward. But all in good time.'

Over the next few sessions, when Kavya was finally able to recount her memory in detail, she started seeing how Dahlia was right about giving up the responsibility. There were a lot of tears and self-loathing, but she eventually started feeling more distant from the event. It was like she was setting herself free by putting it out there. The day she told her the last bits of the night, including her escape to Riya's place, she sobbed for more than half of the session.

'How do you feel now that you have finally shared your experience?'

Composing herself, Kavya replied with a newfound resoluteness.

'It happened, and now it's out there. It's not my terrible secret to keep anymore. I have been denying it, even to myself. A voice inside my head said to me over and over again that nothing happened and I was overreacting. It had been trying to belittle me for feeling so affected. But it's different now. I know what I have been through, and it is a lot. I was not raped, but it was fucking traumatic.'

As Dahlia offered her more tissues, Kavya wiped her face and desperately tried to regain her composure.

'Is this going to give me another closure, Dahlia?' she asked as she continued wiping her face clean.

'We will get there. First, it's imperative to address your feelings around it. Do you still feel guilty or the need to blame?'

'I do, but I also see that it's false. As you suggested, I am going to actively stop this train of thought when it assails me … by recognising the pattern.'

'What will you do to "rewire" your brain and help you stop the pattern?'

'The attack happened to me, not because of me. That will be my focus. I will continuously repeat it to myself till the impulse to blame subsides.'

Dahlia smiled approvingly and closed the diary. Kavya instinctively looked at the clock, and indeed, her hour was going to be up.

'I keep wanting to blame him, though. It makes me feel better.' She said the words desperately, as if she did not want to be left alone with them.

'In some cases, forgiving makes people feel a lot better. I am not suggesting you do, especially if you don't feel ready, but it's just something to think about.'

'How am I going to do that?'

'It could be a long road. But you can start by living in the present. When you react to a current situation, do it with awareness. You will get to know where exactly your past self is interfering. Initially, that observation would be enough, and gradually, you may start to act on it.'

As Kavya made her way to the door, lost in contemplation about Dahlia's words, she heard the therapist calling her name again.

'Have you heard of support groups? It's nothing fancy, just a group of people with a similar traumatic experience getting together and talking about it in a safe place. It has proven to be very useful with some of my previous clients. I will text you a couple of addresses.'

'Thanks, Dahlia,' Kavya responded with genuine gratitude, feeling hopeful for the first time in years.

She started believing she was better as more time went by. More than six months had passed since her outburst with Darsh. He had not got in touch, and Kavya was glad he hadn't. Deciding to remain focused on her recovery, she extended her break from work to a year. Taking Dahlia's advice, she also made it a habit to practise awareness while reacting to any situation in day-to-day interactions. She started trying to resist the patterns in her behaviour that belied her as a trauma victim, even if it meant feeling uncomfortable.

Convinced that Kavya was doing better and had moved out of the self-harm phase, Trisha finally moved out, but came to see her every other day. The first night alone was difficult for her, but she ensured that she faced her demons without any help. She used the breathing techniques that she had picked up in the support group she had been frequenting after Dahlia's suggestion.

The group had inspired a good amount of strength in her. She knew there were many like her, and there was so much to learn from every individual's way of dealing. Additionally, talking about what happened to her several times had somehow taken away the sting of the incident. Gradually, after nearly ten months of therapy, the shame and guilt associated with her assault had disappeared, and Kavya was learning to think of it as a story of survival—an escape and a fight that she could be proud of.

Even though she was stoked about her progress, Kavya knew that the biggest aftermath of the incident was far from solved. Dahlia had told her that the next session would cover her aversion to sex.

She remembered starkly how it was to be around Darsh when she was nineteen. The butterflies in her tummy, the wetness between her legs, the quickening of her heartbeat. But when she raked her brains for anything similar post that night, her mind drew a complete blank. Even when Darsh arrived back in her life, she couldn't feel any desire for him. And it wasn't because he had lost his sex appeal. Yet, it did feel a little different to be around him in the latter days.

There were fleeting moments when she had wanted to reach out and touch him. The mystery as to why his hugs did not bother her was still to be solved. Whatever it was, she needed to talk about it to Dahlia, who could help her figure out what it meant. But before that, she needed to talk to Trisha and tell her everything. That was going to be the litmus test of her progress. When they met next at a café, Kavya was ready to share her secrets with her.

Trisha arrived in a pair of shorts and a colourful bohemian top, announcing her arrival with the sound of her jangling bangles, pushing open the heavy café door. She smiled brightly as she spotted Kavya and made her way to her.

'You look great. I love this therapist! I miss you at work, though.'

'I needed this time off. It's working wonders for me.'

'I am so glad to hear that. We will soon be going out together, you know,' Trisha said just as the waiter arrived to take her order.

After Trisha updated her with bits of office gossip, they got back to discussing Kavya's progress with the therapy.

'By the way, have I thanked you yet for being my rock even when I have kept most of my life in the dark?'

'Oh, so we are going to go all formal now?' Trisha replied flippantly, shrugging off the acknowledgement.

'I mean, I am ready to let you in, Trisha. I want to tell you why I am the way I am, why being around Darsh was problematic for me, and why I overdid the drinks and the pills that night. I want to talk about everything.'

As Kavya bared it all for the first time in an informal setting, she was surprised at how the recounting affected her very little now. It was as if the hurt had lost its sharp edges, vaguely uncomfortable and prickly but bearable. She saw Trisha getting overwhelmed, though, grasping at words while her eyes turned moist.

'To think I made so many jokes about you being cold and sexless.'

Kavya smiled generously. 'You can give me a big hug and make up for it.'

In response, Trisha jumped up from her chair and smothered her in a bear hug. Kavya closed her eyes and resisted pushing her away. Taking a long breath in, she reminded herself that this was safe. Her claustrophobia was just a harmless result of the memories of the force inflicted on her.

'It's OK,' she repeated to herself.

Thirty

'So, let's talk a little bit about your growing years again. I know you have already told me a lot about your life back then, but let's go over some of it again. How would you describe your years in your hometown? Was there ….sort of a defining emotion for you when you grew up?'

'Anxiety. I was very emotional. I still am, I think. But back then I was overthinking all the time and worrying about something or the other. Looking back, I was actually prone to anxiety. It didn't take much for me to panic even then … I was always known as a nervous wreck.'

'Did it make it worse when you realised you were in love with someone so emotionally unavailable?'

Kavya could still feel the heart-stabbing pain his lack of response had caused her for years.

'It was heart-breaking, literally. I was always going back and forth between trying to get him to reciprocate and trying to avoid him… Every time I wanted to move on, there would be some kind of hope which wouldn't let me … looking back, it was nothing short of torture…'

'What about now?' Dahlia asked quietly.

'What about now?' she repeated robotically.

'When he was here with you, did you feel any of that helpless, out-of-control love for him?'

'Of course not. I told you, I hated him most of the time. I asked him to get out of my house!'

'Yes. So, he no longer poses a threat to your emotional stability?'

'Not anymore. To be honest, he did initially ... because of all that unexpressed hurt and anger I had for him. But not anymore. I have told him what I wanted to, and I would like to think I am over it. He does not mean much except for being a part of my childhood.'

'OK, let's go back to your childhood again. Was it acceptable for young people to go out on dates, etc.?'

'No. It happened, but in secrecy, and most parents never knew.'

'How did you look at your classmates who were having relationships? How did you feel about that?'

'I thought it was wrong. I had a strong sense of right and wrong, as anyone in a small town does, especially a girl. I thought it was wrong and tried to avoid those people.'

'So, when you realised you were attracted to Darsh—sexually attracted, specifically—how did it make you feel about yourself?'

Faced with this question, Kavya felt a strong need to justify herself even after so many years, and jumped to defend herself.

'It was different with him. We were best friends, and I was in love with him for years before I started feeling those things. Even when I decided to sleep with him, it was more for his sake. I was trying to save him from becoming someone he was not.'

Kavya told her about reading *The Stranger* and how it had influenced her into doing what she did.

'I see a conflict here, Kavya. You have told me time and again that you felt a strong desire for him, and yet, when you did try to sleep with him, you say it was for his sake.'

Kavya nodded but chose not to look Dahlia in the eye. Her eyes unnerved her at times.

She heard an almost inaudible sigh and raised her head slightly to see Dahlia switching her crossed legs from right over left to left over right.

'OK, let's do a small exercise now. Can you close your eyes for me?'

She did as told, and Dahlia's voice floated towards her hypnotically.

'Now take a deep breath in and then out. Yes. Another one. Good. One more.

'Let's go back into your past to the time that your feelings started bothering you. Watch Kavya on her bad days, but from a distance. It's vital to remember that you are watching from afar, as a thirty-plus woman. You are not her anymore. You can do that?'

'Yes.'

'Watch and tell me what made her cry on the particular days that are running through your mind. What exactly did anyone do to cause her to feel so miserable? Who hurt her and when?'

Almost reflexively, Kavya started scouring through all her memories to find the things that Darsh had done to cause her suffering. But as her breath relaxed under Dahlia's calming voice, and she navigated through the maze of her memories, she found that trespassing on her younger self gave her a different vantage point.

Scenes flashed through her mind's screen at Dahlia's behest. She saw herself clinging to him on his bike while returning from Jeeva Lake, and how he had asked her to move back when they reached the town. It was because she had told him it was important for her not to be seen with him. She saw herself asking him why he had kissed her.

'Didn't you ask me to?' he'd said simply, unable to see it meant more to her.

She saw herself going drunk to his house and falling into his arms, and all he did was tuck her into bed. For the first time, she could see herself as a clueless teenager whose love was entirely one-sided and selfish. In contrast, Darsh—who was always open about not feeling anything for anyone—had taken care not to hurt her, even in his limited capacity.

Kavya could feel tears pricking at the corners of her eyes as she confessed the tough things she saw, keeping her eyes closed.

'I was attracted to him, but it was one-sided. He fit the bill perfectly. He was older, physically attractive and unattainable. I was convinced I had something special going on with him because we were friends, but it was just me wanting it to be something special. I couldn't compare my feelings to the other girls who chased after him because I judged them. I looked down on Riya's obsession as ridiculous. I couldn't attribute my feelings to just a crush or an attraction, it had to be special and deep. But I don't know now.'

As Kavya paused, Dahlia gave her a moment to digest the new perspective and said slowly, 'Not knowing is a good thing.'

Kavya opened her eyes then and accepted her responsibility for her misery.

'He grew up without love, and I knew perfectly well that he did not understand it. It was not his fault that I kept expecting him to understand my feelings and reciprocate. Even though he was extremely cold to everyone else, he always tried to indulge me as much as he could. He saw his mother because I asked him to. He kept all my meetings with him discreet because I did not want anyone to know. He tucked me safely in bed when I crashed his place drunk and unannounced in the middle of the night. I kept reading a possibility of love in everything he did because of my stubbornness, but he never once acted in any way that could mislead me into thinking he could love me back.

'It's great that you are taking responsibility for your feelings. Must be a freeing feeling, right?'

'It feels like I am finally able to set both of us free...'

'That's a good start. Would you like to go further, Kavya? We can stop if it gets too overwhelming.'

'No, I want to go further,' Kavya said, squeezing her eyes together again, waiting for Dahlia's voice to lead her further into her dark areas.

'Watch her when she prepares to ask him to sleep with her. What exactly is her state of mind? Is she uncomfortable with that thought?'

A mild shock passed through Kavya at the prospect of confronting that part of her life. It was the most outrageous thing she had done in her entire life, with disastrous results—an action that had changed her life forever. Her legs trembled slightly as she prepared to face her reasons for doing what she did. Was it a foolish impulse or an act of love? She slowly walked herself through the days leading to her birthday, once the idea had germinated in her mind.

She saw the excitement in her younger self, a type of daring frenzy that she did not realise she was capable of. She saw the dreaminess in her eyes when she dared to go and buy herself the lacy lingerie. She saw her glazed eyes as she lay awake, imagining how it would be to lie under him. She saw the hesitation about the moral implications of her actions slip away as the day approached. She could not see her characteristic doubtfulness and nervousness, but a determined focus on achieving her goal. She was not herself. Something strange had taken over her, and Kavya struggled to put a name to it. It was not an act of compassion to rescue him. It was not even love, as the constant wistful pining had disappeared.

'Lust,' Kavya said out loud, finally labelling what she saw.

'It was lust, and I was ashamed of it,' she spoke, her voice communicating her surprise at this discovery. 'The only reason I was there was to gratify myself.'

Kavya opened her eyes again with that realisation, as years of victimhood crumbled under the pressure of the discovery that her action was born out of her desire. It had nothing to do with Darsh. Fresh tears rushed to fill her eyes as she saw Dahlia looking at her with compassion.

'He was unable to maintain deeper relationships. I needed to make a choice: to move on or to indulge my sexual attraction. But I couldn't accept that I wanted to sleep with him for my sake. It would mean I was morally corrupt. The book gave me a cover to exercise my impulses without feeling bad about it.'

She was sobbing again. Dahlia handed her the tissues again and interjected.

'That's impressive hindsight. Of course, you know now that desire is nothing to be ashamed of, but a natural impulse.'

'Yes, I know that now. It was never about him, was it? He never did anything to either inspire those feelings in me or to encourage them. He was just who he was, a flawed youth dealing with things his way.'

'Let's move forward. What happens when this desire is not gratified? How does young Kavya feel once she doesn't know what to do with the raging hormones inside?'

Kavya closed her eyes again and saw her younger self walking away in the thick of the night like a maniac.

'I am fighting with this weird frustration, which is more physical than emotional. I want to get rid of this feverishness because it makes me feel dirty. That's why I can't stop walking at that mad pace without thinking where I am going. My body seems like it's on fire.'

Kavya took a short pause to gather herself, with tears trickling down in anticipation of what was going to happen.

'I am blaming myself for expressing my desire as I walk around. I feel dirty for wanting him.'

There was silence as Kavya stopped talking after that, focusing her energy on facing the assault again. Even though she had now talked about it multiple times, she was re-living it in Dahlia's office today, with closed eyes. It was an intense experience and she spoke through gritted teeth as she spelt out how that felt.

'And in that state of mind, I am being forcefully touched and hit and assaulted. My body hurts but it's my mind that sort of freezes. Even when this monster runs away, I don't do anything for minutes because...'

She stopped short of completing the sentence, too stunned to mouth the words.

Her whole body was taut as if she were resisting a physical force, and she even squeezed her eyes tighter to stop the fresh tears from rolling down her face. They did anyway.

'Because?' Dahlia repeated tenderly. It was not a question but an encouragement to let it out.

And Kavya did. Her voice came out trembling, even broken.

'Because I feel ... I feel like a stupid bitch who deserved it.'

Followed by those words, the silence in the room seemed jarring. The answer to her sexual aversion hung in the air, revealed and exposed. Her world went deathly still as one more knot came undone. A feeling of weightlessness descended on her and she opened her eyes. Dahlia was looking at her with an unchanged expression.

'It was clear to me. I was punished for wanting to have sex. My desire for Darsh was wrong. If I did not want something so wrong, there would have been no rejection, no hurt, no attack. I would have been home safe.'

'It does seem that you have been living your life by a rule made by a heartbroken adolescent girl who had no idea how to protect herself anymore. She decided not wanting to have sex will keep her safe. Is that how you still see it?'

Kavya shook her head, wiping her nose.

'Then it might be time to take over your life from her.'

Leaving Dahlia's office that day, Kavya believed that a little room in her heart might have been left unscarred. Her sessions had transformed her piece by piece, but this last one put her in touch with a warm cove inside her that she hadn't known still existed. With this acceptance of her past as a whole came a sense of responsibility that relieved the heavy load of victimhood she had been carrying around for twelve years. As she owned up to her weaknesses and her strengths as a growing girl, she could do so for others as well. She started seeing Darsh as a separate identity who had little part to play in her life. He had been dealing with his own demons in the best possible way he thought he could.

Most importantly, the last moments of the session had laid bare a truth she had been running away from. It had been her choice to avoid sex. Knowing this, she was ready to try to flip her choice. As a grown woman, she had agency—and there was nothing to stop her from using it.

A month down the line, Kavya surprised herself by booking a ticket to go to Parvatnagar. She had avoided that town like the plague, even when her father still worked at the mill and stayed in the same flat with her mother. Despite multiple demands by them to visit, she could not bring herself to go back. That town reminded her of nothing but pain and carried a terrifying potential to trigger the worst in her. But now, she wanted to face her fears, encouraged by the progress she had made with her therapy. If she could renew her ties to the town, she could really call herself normal again. It was too strong a temptation to resist. Her mother was ecstatic at the news. She had never liked Bangalore, unable to stay there for more than a few days at a time.

When she met Dahlia next, Kavya was given an approving smile upon sharing her intention to visit Parvatnagar, but she was also offered a note of caution.

'Well, this makes me believe you are really doing well. Keep in mind, though, that recovery is not a race and most of it happens on a subconscious level over time. So, do what seems natural to you, pushing your boundaries at a comfortable pace.'

'I feel certain about this. I don't want to run away anymore.'

Dahlia nodded in approval.

'Dahlia…' She cleared her throat, preparing to bring up the one thing that still perplexed her. 'Why do you think Darsh's touch does not make me uncomfortable?'

In return, however, she was presented with another question.

'Tell me, Kavya, did you mind your mother's touch after the incident? Or even Riya's when you stayed with her? Did their hands, when they held you or touched you, remind you of the incident?'

While contemplating the answer, Kavya, to her surprise, realised she had developed an aversion to touch once she had moved away from Parvatnagar.

'I think Darsh, like your mom, is part of your trusted circle. He came to you from the past, from that time when you were unscarred by your violent experience.'

'But I had hated him for so many years, blaming him for everything when he came back.'

'That's in your mind. However, what we are talking about is a physiological reaction of your body. Your mind may have been conflicted about him; your body probably was not. It could happen.'

Kavya felt emboldened by this information and told Dahlia about the last couple of days around him. 'You know, there were moments when it did feel like I was almost normal around him. In fact, a few times, I almost wanted to touch him myself,' Kavya confessed, thinking of the charged moment when he had held her close during their midnight chat and the morning after when he had stopped to chat while returning from his run.

'Well, if you are able to feel physically normal and your body shows a capacity to respond, even on an unconscious level, I would consider that a promising sign.'

Thirty-One

After a long and tiring flight, Kavya hired a cab for the final two-hour ride to Parvatnagar. Even though the town had an airport now, the flights were few and far between, and none connected to Bangalore. She would not have minded the car ride, though, as the route was quite scenic but the only cab available was old and smelly and rattled noisily at every bump on the road.

In an attempt to distract herself from the unpleasantness of her ride and the horrendous music the driver was playing, Kavya leaned out the window and let the wind beat across her face as they rode at high speed. Trisha had moved into her place while she was gone, and Kavya had left a detailed care guide for her plants. Even though Trisha had repeatedly assured her that her garden wouldn't be neglected, Kavya still planned to call her every day to remind her not to forget to water them or to spend some time talking to them.

They entered Parvatnagar's periphery at dusk. The sun had just gone down, and the chain of hills she knew so well stood resplendent against a skyline splattered with hues of orange. Despite its sorry shape, the cab zipped by them impressively and soon rattled along the tiny road running through the Parvatnagar jungle.

Kavya felt that familiar sinking sensation rise in her tummy, but she tried to observe this event like a witness. She acknowledged the unpleasantness but distanced her mind from it, and just as Dahlia had promised, it passed after a few minutes of difficulty. Coming back to her surroundings, she noticed they had started the uphill drive that would take them to the town. As they manoeuvred through the series of hairpin turns amidst the picturesque valley, the finality of what she had done dawned on her. She would be face to face with everything she had been running from. A glimpse of Jeeva Lake, still and quiet after sunset, unsettled her as the car raced past it.

The town was more crowded than she remembered. Even after sunset the marketplace was buzzing with activity, and new structures had sprung up everywhere, such as malls and office buildings. Once they reached the residential area, the cab drove through the colonies of similar-looking residences that continued housing steel factory officials. Soon, she was crossing the white bungalow. There it was, still looking grossly incongruous amid the small identical duplexes. She felt a slight movement in her heart, but it disappeared quickly. The past didn't matter; the future did.

After a lengthy dinner with her parents, Kavya climbed up to her erstwhile room. Her mother insisted she sleep downstairs as her room was now more of a storeroom, but she refused. Other than looking tinier and smelling like a place that hadn't seen sunlight for long, the room was liveable. She opened the window to let some air in, and her eyes fell on the Purohit bungalow shed. It looked long abandoned, with the door hanging off the hinges, and Kavya wondered if they still had staff to look after the huge property that was evidently not in its prime anymore. She was aware that no one lived there anymore, as Darsh's father had died in the US a few years ago while living with his son.

She opened the tiny wooden cupboard to check if her things had been cleared out, but was surprised that most of her clothes were untouched. As she rummaged through her old wardrobe, something flopped with a thud. She picked up a tattered book that had lain inside unnoticed for years: *The Stranger,* the one that had changed her life. Some of the pages had been eaten by termites, producing a series of tiny holes along the sides.

She put it on her desk and then changed the bedsheets to settle in for a good night's sleep. The journey had been long, and she dozed off soon, thinking how nice and relaxed she felt at home, contrary to what she had expected. She spent the next day doing nothing, relaxing around the house and taking short walks in the neighbourhood. However, by evening, her mother was fielding calls from many around the town, curious as news of Kavya's return spread.

She sat back on the sofa, switching channels, amused at her mother's exaggerated praise for her successful career and financial status. A sense of pride sneaked through as she remembered how much it had always meant to her that she build a life exactly like she had. A few of them started dropping by gradually, and Kavya met everyone politely, letting her mother steer the conversation.

The next day, soon after breakfast, her mother handed her mobile phone to Kavya, announcing it was Riya on the line. Kavya had lost touch with her over the years. They had drifted apart when Riya got married and pregnant in quick succession. There wasn't much to discuss as their lives became diametrically opposite. But with the news that she was back in town, Riya quickly arranged to meet her, seemingly excited about catching up.

As the venue for their meeting was a café in the central market, Kavya finally willed herself to venture outside her immediate neighbourhood's comfort zone. She walked to the marketplace in a sweatshirt and an old pair of jeans, wishing to avoid scrutiny. She was not used to it anymore, and smiling at every face was getting tiring. However, as she walked, she realised she was inviting stares. It could have been anything. She was "new" to the town or the way she dressed was different to what town people were used to, but it placed an irrational fear in her heart that everyone knew what had happened to her. She quickly smothered that thought, identifying it as a 'trigger thought' in Dahlia's words.

As Kavya approached the designated café, she spotted her friend right away. She was sitting at one of the foremost tables, scrolling on her phone, looking bored, but her eyes lit up instantly when she glanced up and saw Kavya. Intending to smother her with a hug, Riya rushed towards her but stopped short of the embrace when she noticed Kavya's discomfort. Feeling instantly contrite about her coldness, Kavya gave her a short, awkward hug. To her surprise, it did not make her queasy. She was reminded of Dahlia's conjecture. Most probably, the aversion was to people who came into her life after the assault. Or maybe she was already recovering?

Even after a decade of virtually no contact, the conversation flowed like there never was a pause in their friendship. Riya launched into a detailed account of her life. Her parents had given her their family house and had bought a property in a neighbouring town, so she lived in the same house but with her husband and kids. She confessed she did not have much to complain about except for the ten kilos she had gained over time as a mother. Kavya reminded her earnestly that weight was the last thing she should worry about when her life was so full and she was healthy and happy.

Eventually, Riya addressed the elephant in the room by asking Kavya how she was doing.

Kavya started giving her a list of her professional milestones, and Riya rolled her eyes. She stated that, thanks to her mother, the whole of Parvatnagar knew her salary, profit margins and company scale.

'Maybe you should hire your mom for marketing!'

They laughed, and then Riya asked again, gently touching Kavya's hand. It was then Kavya spotted the faint scar on Riya's wrist from that time in their childhood and flipped the question back to her.

'I am so glad family now surrounds you. You don't get impulses to hurt yourself anymore like this, do you?'

'I am glad about my family, too, Kavya. My boring but reliable husband and evil yet adorable children pull me back from all dark thoughts. It was a different time back then. My folks made me feel lonely, but now my family fulfils me.'

Kavya nodded in response, feeling happy for her.

'What about you? You don't plan to get married ever or what?' Riya asked, bringing the focus back to Kavya.

'I haven't planned anything at all. It's just not top of mind right now.'

'But you are OK, right? You have put everything that happened in the past? Tell me that's nothing to do with you living like a nun.'

Kavya took a long moment before replying. Her impulse was to deny it all, but she had learnt to talk about her feelings through therapy last year, and Riya deserved her honesty.

'I am not OK, but I am getting there. I feel better about myself. I can talk about it now. And I feel there's some hope for me after all.'

Riya reached for Kavya's hand across the table and squeezed it.

'I am so glad. But trust me, you are not missing out on anything! This marriage thing is a boring business. Men! Super overrated!'

Kavya laughed. It was obvious that Riya's talent for exaggeration hadn't worn out. In the pause that ensued, she decided to tell Riya about Darsh. It did seem like a natural thing to reveal to her at this point.

'By the way, talking about overrated men,' Kavya started with a deliberate nonchalance in her voice. 'You know who was in Bangalore last year? Darsh Purohit. He rang me up out of nowhere.'

Riya's jaw practically dropped. Kavya anticipated the shock, as there had always been an unsaid block on mentioning the D-word between them post that night.

'Yes, he was there for some time and he even apologised for, you know, the past.'

Riya looked flabbergasted, and it took her a minute to find her voice, but when she did, Kavya was surprised at her response.

'So it bloody worked?' Riya almost spoke to herself, and Kavya felt the hair on her hand rise at her tone.

'What worked?' she asked.

Riya took her hand in hers in response, and Kavya started feeling a little uncomfortable.

'So I did not tell you this because, you know… But Darsh came to town a few years ago. To disperse his father's ashes! Can you imagine? Darsh, flying all the way for a ritual? I couldn't believe it too.'

'And?'

'So, I ran into him, and I was quite unprepared. Well, you know me, my anger took the best of me and I kind of screamed at him: that he was scum or something to that effect. And you would think he would just ignore me, like he used to, right? But surprise! he comes up closer and acknowledges me. "Riya, right?" he says, and then casually lowers himself to say hi to my son!

'Then he straightens up and looks back at me and says he's sorry if he hurt me in the past. And I stop him right there. And I say no … no, it's not for me, you arrogant SOB, it's for Kavya.

'And as I mention you, this whole air changes. I swear I see him literally stiffen. Anyways, I turn away in disgust and anger, but he stops me and asks, "Where's Kavya now?"

'I got so angry, I couldn't wait to storm off. And I did. But he called me later that evening and asked to meet.

I am not very proud of it, but I met him. The lure of seeing him regret everything was too much. And please don't get mad … but I could not help telling him about what happened that night, after he sent you away. It just seemed unfair that he could live so guilt-free. I really wanted to make him feel bad!'

They both turned silent after that, the flow of conversation drying up. The news hit Kavya like a bucket of ice-cold water. She had wondered a thousand times why Darsh had turned up in her life, but it never occurred to her that he knew. The only people who knew were her mother and Riya. She could not foresee a scenario where he could meet them without her knowledge. But it had happened, and even as she processed this information, the last events started falling into place like a puzzle that was solving itself. Assuring Riya mechanically that she was OK, she returned home in a suspended state of contemplation, not letting the feelings overwhelm her.

So, it was guilt that brought him to Bangalore. Not his work, not his philanthropy, but guilt. He stayed near her and unsettled her on purpose. He must have known she was not OK. After all, he studied people for a living. He forced her to face the facts by bringing the past into her house. He must have intentionally taken her to the forest that night to check if she could handle it. All this while, he was counting on a breakdown, which would either free her from her demons or push her towards an active path of recovery.

She was angry. On a deeper level, she understood that he wanted to help, and he most certainly succeeded, but she was angry nonetheless. She had been kept in the dark. In this state of confusion, Kavya decided to finally mention the D-word to her mother when they sat together for evening tea after she reached home.

'Do you know I met Darsh in Bangalore, Maa?' she asked, trying to sound casual, drumming her fingers on the wooden dining table as her mother made tea.

'What was he doing in Bangalore? He hasn't been to this town in over a decade, except once! Neglected his father's lifetime of legacy… Have you seen the shambles their property is in?'

It was clear that not much had changed in the department of her mother's feelings towards Darsh. She would probably want to kill him if she knew the full story. Kavya felt that old urge to defend him surfacing again, forgetting the anger she was feeling.

'He has changed a lot.'

Her mother poured the tea quietly into two cups and brought it to the dining table without betraying any reaction.

'I also want to tell you something else. I was in therapy for the last year, and he may have had something to do with it.'

This shocked her mother visibly, and she opened her mouth to launch a flurry of questions. But Kavya cut her off.

'I was doing OK. It was just to let go of, you know, those memories.'

'But how would talking to a stranger help you when all these years did not make you forget?'

'Not talking to a stranger, talking to a qualified professional who specialises in retraining your brain…'

'So, it helped? Are you ready to at least try to get married?'

Kavya drew in an exasperated breath.

'What is it with you and marriage!'

'That's the only thing you are running away from. Everything else is sorted in your life. So, it does not mean anything to me if your therapy did not make you change your mind about marriage.'

'It did help. I am not there yet, but I am getting there,' Kavya acquiesced grudgingly, and saw her mother's face break into an impromptu smile.

'I have some leads that I want to explore. I will forward you the profiles.'

'I said I am not there yet.'

'These things don't happen overnight. You have to start somewhere. And why was Purohit in Bangalore?'

'I don't know, but he kind of reminded me that life was more than routine. But hey, you don't have to hate him. He is not a big deal to me anymore.'

'He better not be. You behaved like he was a magnet, losing all sense when it came to him. You should never let anyone have that kind of power over you.'

Kavya finished her tea quietly and made her way up to her room. She had a lot on her mind and did not need to continue this conversation. At the same time, she knew her mother always had a point, even if she had a very annoying way of putting it forward. But it was different now, wasn't it? She had control. He was still important, in a weird, unexplainable way – therapy had made that much clear – but she valued her life and her well-being more.

Thirty-Two

She wanted to stay angry at Darsh but had run out of reasons. Something had flared up in her when Riya told her that Darsh knew it all, but it fizzled out as she considered the circumstances. It was an entirely reasonable step on his part not to have told her before, as it could have led to devastating results. But now she started wondering what made him come halfway around the world to face the consequences of an action that no one knew about. Why would he make all that effort for her to heal, the need for which even she was unaware? Why, if not because he cared deeper than he let on? Any residue of anger she might have had for him dissipated like fog off some placid lake at that thought.

Amidst these swirling thoughts, Kavya tried calling it an early night but could not sleep. She tossed and turned in her bed, fighting restlessness. She wanted to let him know that she knew. She had so much to say now that all the curtains between them were taken down. She picked up her mobile phone and scrolled to his name but stopped short of pressing the call button. She didn't even have his US number. What would she tell him even if she had it? She put the phone back on the side table, where she spotted *The Stranger* lying innocently, which made her even more restless.

Her window was half open, and she pushed the pane wider to inspect Purohit's premises. It was the start of winter, and the air that gushed inside was chilly. The whole area was plunged into darkness, but she had seen earlier how the gardens around the mansion had turned into a wilderness, the reason behind the stagnant scent of green in the night air.

She remembered how the sleek marble path leading to the house had disappeared beneath a thick layer of haphazard vegetation, and the paint on the house had started to come off. It seemed he had not even cared to employ a caretaker to keep this place going. What a pity! It was such a magnificent building with so much elegance. The utter stillness beyond the wall started haunting her as happier memories from her childhood flashed through her mind. Their first meeting, the summer afternoons when he taught her weird tricks, the evening rides and the tuition before exams—all snippets from the past managed to resurface in Kavya's consciousness now that she had released the unpleasant ones.

But what use was it now? She had asked him to leave, confessing she hated him. And he had. This deserted building about to fall into ruins was a testimony to the fate of their friendship. Dead and abandoned. Feeling sad, she turned to climb back into bed. It was then that she heard a distant sound of a motorbike approaching. Minutes after the sound ceased, she heard the familiar squeak of iron as the gates opened. Someone had come to visit the bungalow. Kavya jumped to get back to the window, her heart racing at this unexpected development with hope in her heart, and peered down just in time to watch Darsh glide in on a motorcycle, cutting through the thick undergrowth of ferns like they did not even exist.

Her first urge was to cry at this coincidence, followed by another to run to him. But calming herself, she went back and buried herself in her bed. What good had this spontaneity done her in the past? She could pretend she did not know he was in town and fall asleep. But after staring at her clock for half an hour waiting to fall asleep, she abandoned the effort to stomp on the rising will to see him.

Taken over by the same impulsiveness that she had lived to regret, she picked up *The Stranger* and opened the back door of her room to climb down the steps. Jumping the wall, she walked to the house quickly, urgently, keeping her eyes glued to the ground, too scared to look around. The darkness and the forest-like scent made her skin crawl with fear. The cold wind did not make it easier. Thankfully, she had put on a warm pullover instinctively before stepping out. She had a long way to go before she could make peace with darkness, but she made it to the building because of the adrenaline in her system.

The door to the house was open, and she stepped in quietly, fighting the memories of her birthday night that crept back into her head. Reminding herself she was in control this time, she progressed towards the living room: the only room with some lights on.

The room was as she remembered. The bungalow might have looked unkempt, but it was spotlessly maintained from the inside. She took it all in like the last time she was here. The huge ornate mirrors, the antique furniture, and the bright Persian rug below the swinging chandelier were resplendent as ever. Then her eyes fell on the sofa. Darsh was sprawled on it, asleep. His tall frame made even the huge sofa look slightly cramped. His feet, running out of space, hung carelessly over the armrest. An open book was resting on his chest. It looked like he had dozed off minutes ago while reading. The fireplace was crackling with what seemed like a freshly made fire, heating the room the old-fashioned way. Even though days were not particularly cold, the temperature dropped quickly at night, even more so on his premises.

She was standing in the same place where all her misery was rooted. Did she want to be here? An intense fear of being sucked back into the quicksand of her issues struck her, but then she spotted herself in the large hanging mirror on the opposite wall. She was a grown woman now, not the girl afraid and helpless against her longing. There was a significant difference between yesterday and today. She was focused on herself at this moment, not on anyone else. It didn't matter what Darsh thought or didn't. She was here to tell him she had forgiven him and herself.

'Kavya?' She heard his voice cut through her reverie and turned swiftly, pulling the shutters down on her fears. He sat up in a quick, lithe move without taking his eyes off her, surprise written all over his face. His hair was cropped shorter than she remembered from a year ago, and he looked leaner, somehow younger.

There were questions. Wasn't he supposed to be in the US? Why had he come back to Parvatnagar? How come nobody knew about it? But she parked them all in her mind as she walked towards him and took a seat, determined to have the conversation she came here for.

'Here, I wanted to return this to you,' she said, handing him the worn-out book.

He took it from her hand, flipped through it gingerly and then raised his eyes at her questioningly.

'It was creepy of me to sneak into your house that night. In part, this made me do it,' she said, pointing at the book. 'But essentially, it was because I wanted to. So what happened after I left was not your fault.'

She saw recognition dawning on his face as he realised she knew that he knew. His eyes turned softer, almost afraid.

'Neither were you obligated to sleep with me just because I asked you to, nor could you have known what would happen later, so stop feeling guilty.'

He averted his eyes as she finished, and for the first time, Kavya saw the pain of guilt appear on his face. He looked down at the book and continued flipping the pages, avoiding looking at her.

'Darsh, I mean it,' she said.

He raised his eyes, and she saw turbulence on his impassive face for the first time. He was fighting the frustration rising in him. When he spoke, his voice came out quiet but firm.

'I should have known how upset you would get. I could have predicted your reaction. I could have stopped you from running out into the night. I could have done a lot of things. I could have had the sense not to open the door to that girl when you were still inside. Nothing, absolutely nothing, will change the fact that I was fucking someone whose name I don't even remember while you were being assaulted under the threat of a damn knife.'

Silence followed the strongly worded confession, and the only sound was the fire crackling in the corner as they both looked away. Something akin to anger thrummed through her veins again, but she ignored it and chose to feed her forgiving side. His downcast features made her feel sorry for him. It was not every day that Darsh showed emotion. She had imagined for years that seeing him suffer would assuage her, but right then, all she felt was a strong impulse to make it all right. So she went off-script.

'Give me that book,' she said, and as soon as he handed it to her, she threw it into the flames. Hungrily, the flames lapped at it, and her rising anger and hurt dissipated.

Darsh inched closer to her and slowly rested his head on her shoulder. For a change, there was an unsaid need for comfort from his side, and he seemed to be trying to seek it from her. As they stared at the fire together, she was overcome with a certain contentment. Maybe it was possible to bury all their history after all and start afresh.

'There's a little bit that I want to thank you for, too. I met one of the therapists from your list, and it worked wonders. I feel good about where I am now.'

He raised his head and looked at her with new interest.

'That is why you came back to town ... the past is beginning to lose its power over you...'

'I came here to test if the past has already lost power over me. And so far so good.'

This time, it was her who nestled her head in the crook of his arm just as she made that overconfident claim. His arm came up from behind and rested protectively on her shoulder. A tiny part inside her chided her. Was she really making progress or just deluding herself with short-term adrenaline? But then, wasn't his arm, wrapped around her, proof that she was normal? Or that she could hope to be normal one day? It was time she told him.

'Darsh, there is something I need to tell you,' she murmured without moving. He smelt of fresh mint and radiated a warmth that Kavya didn't want to be deprived of anymore. But as soon as she uttered these words, he shifted. The movement was almost sudden, as if he couldn't wait to put some distance between them. The spell was broken. She raised her head and looked at him questioningly.

'Kavya, I am moving back ... to SF, for good.' He announced, completely out of the blue.

Thirty-Three

Kavya did not know what to make of that information at that moment, but she realised she couldn't tell him about her struggles with human touch now. That moment had somehow slipped away. As she thought of an appropriate response, her eyes darted towards the dying fire, which seemed to signal that her purpose of the visit was over. The room felt cold, and so did her heart.

'It's such a great improvement that you are telling me that.' With a hollow laugh, she quipped coldly and got up quietly before adding resolutely, 'I better go back.'

He stood up as well, hands digging deep into his pockets.

'Can I see you off? To the wall?'

She looked up at him. Anxiety, guilt, and fear were written all over his face, even though he was trying to be stoic. Seeing how the balance seemed reversed from the last time was almost endearing. He seemed to be walking on eggshells around her while she felt like she had nothing to lose anymore. She did not hesitate to laugh at the irony and told him exactly what she thought was running in his mind to have him ask her that question.

'Why? So that you can see I jump the wall and go home? Still don't give me any credit, do you?'

In response, she just saw his face harden a little, as if he was hurt by her conjecture.

'Maybe, Kavya, it's more because I know you don't like to be alone in the dark? Maybe I just want to spend a few more minutes with you? But you don't give me any credit, do you?'

Kavya acquiesced with a sheepish smile, and they walked out of his bungalow together. As the cold wind slapped their faces, Kavya gave an involuntary shudder. Darsh placed his hand into hers and led her through the lonely stretch of wilderness that was once his manicured garden. Looking around, she spied the new motorbike just ahead of the broken shed, his erstwhile home in his rebellious years. When they finally reached the wall, she turned to steal another look at the bike, feeling strangely unsettled. The steel shone out atrociously amongst the surrounding blackness.

'I rented it for the stay. Driving is still a pain in this godforsaken town,' he offered, noticing her interest.

Kavya gave an absent-minded half-scoff at his comment. A daring idea was already taking over her mind. Had she indeed recovered? Maybe she needed a test? Her subconscious challenged her. But Dahlia said recovery is not a race. But then again, it was the only chance she had to find out. If not tonight, she would never get to work this out again, with him by her side, a qualified professional and a close friend, both combined in one.

'Darsh, could you take me to the jungle? I want to go where it happened.'

The question came out of her like a quick spurt of breath that got released after being held in a little too long. The tone was sharp, sudden and urgent.

Against the moonlit expanse of the sky, she saw his towering profile turn rigid. The street lamps illuminated his face just enough for her to make out that his expression had turned brooding. It was reminiscent of his younger days, when his feelings were often masked with an unfathomable expression on his face.

'It's important for me,' she asserted.

It looked like he was studying her like a subject while he contemplated his answer. She was mildly annoyed at how she had lost the tiny window where he seemed vulnerable and human. After a few agonising seconds, he quietly motioned her towards the bike, signalling his acquiescence. She sat behind him gingerly as he fished out the keys and started the engine. If fear wasn't spreading through her like the threads of a spiderweb, she could have probably better appreciated the fact that she was riding with him after a lifetime.

Kavya tried to quieten her panicking mind as the motorbike glided through the roads. *Remember, you already did it in the Bangalore woods. How peacefully you slept all the way back!* But Bangalore was different. This was the exact place where it happened. Was she overstepping her own boundaries? What if she lost all the recovery she had earned in the past year because of a foolhardy impulse?

She didn't notice immediately when the bike slowed down and came to a halt. It was only when Darsh reached for her hand did she realise how deep her fingernails were digging into his shoulders. He took one of her hands and wrapped it around his waist.

'You are safe. I am not going anywhere.'

With her arms now wrapped around him, she laid her head against his back and said a small yes. She knew she had to calm down for it to work. The ride resumed, and she kept her eyes closed for a while, letting his warmth block out the fear. When they stopped again, and Kavya reluctantly opened her eyes, she saw they had reached the rough trail that led deeper into the forest. From here, walking was the only option.

As they climbed down and he parked the bike, she had a moment of absolute trepidation and wanted to run back. Sensing her agitation, he took her hand quietly, and they moved ahead. Soon, the trail they were walking on disappeared and gave way to the forest floor covered in grass and wet soil. Darsh switched on an old-fashioned flashlight. She hadn't even noticed he was carrying it. He knew the woods like the back of his hand, and it was a moonlit night, but he had probably brought it for her sake.

They walked for a little while before the sound of dry leaves being crushed under their feet told her they had almost reached the spot. Kavya's heartbeat quickened dangerously as she instinctively realised she was right where she was first grabbed. She shot a wild glance at the clearing metres ahead, where he had taken her and pushed her to the ground.

Her hold on Darsh's hand tightened as she started feeling shortness of breath. The scent of the forest suddenly overwhelmed her, reminding her of the horror of the experience. She was beginning to forget Darsh's presence as her brain went into overdrive, producing a flurry of hormones. With their branches growing every which way, the dark trees started closing in on her, and she felt a searing pain in her chest. She felt her knees buckle, and all sounds were blocked except a loud ringing in her ears. But as she slid down, she was suddenly reminded she was not alone, as Darsh's arms came up and enveloped her protectively, breaking her fall.

She started to take in long breaths, gulping at the air. His voice finally reached her ears, but it seemed like he was on the other side of the forest, his words drowned by her pounding heartbeat.

'I've got you, Kavya. Don't let this win. Breathe. Focus. It will pass.'

She closed her eyes and continued breathing, counting her heart rate, waiting for it to slow down. She was safe, she told herself repeatedly. She was not alone. It was not the woods that hurt her. It was not the place that hurt her. She thought of her garden back home, and bright-coloured flowers danced in front of her. And then, as suddenly as it had begun, the attack passed, and she opened her eyes cautiously. The forest stared at her meekly as if conceding defeat, knowing all its theatrics were lost on her. She had fought a powerful attack right in the jungle of Parvatnagar. She knew this would change things for her. It gave her the courage to go on.

'That's where he took me.' She pointed boldly at the clearing ahead as they walked hand in hand to the spot concealed due to thick undergrowth. Darsh let his flashlight shine on the area conveniently hidden by a tall wall of trees. He easily led her there, crossing the barrage of undergrowth and ferns. Being able to step into the exact place she was once dragged to with control made that memory distant and powerless.

'This is where he pushed me down and hit me. His hands—all I remember are his hands, coming down on me, on my mouth, on my face, again and again…' she narrated, as anger started seeping out of her in a steady trickle and soon turned into a roaring gush.

Tears came as the memories of the pain came alive, but she did not hold back. Recounting every move, every feeling and every sensation, she released her trauma back to the surroundings where she had received it. She wiped her tears but more came. She had not cried so much even in Dahlia's office while telling her. Darsh held her close, his hand resting lightly above her waist, in a safe embrace, listening.

'His filthy mouth kept hurting me, biting me … trying to pry my mouth open, but I just couldn't. He took his time, you know, terrorising me, scaring me into thinking what was coming. And then he was on top of me, and I wanted to die, Darsh.'

She sagged against the tree behind her just as those words left her, tired of the overwhelming experience, about to let go and slide down, but he stopped her and pulled her into his arms. Nestled against his chest, she kept crying for a while. He ran his fingers through her hair, aiming to relax her, and she could feel his warmth. It brought up good memories from her younger years when he made her feel comfortable even in his silence. As her sobs quietened, she heard him speak, his voice soothing yet unrelenting, as he directed her to continue.

'Tell me about the part where you fought back.'

Being asked to talk about her fight reminded her that she was a survivor. She walked a few steps ahead and stared hard at the forest floor where she had been pinned mercilessly years ago. Bending down, she ran her hands over the muddy earth.

'I don't know where that sudden zeal came from, but I started kicking and screaming, not caring that he had threatened me with the knife. I survived, but I don't think my sudden helpless scuffle had to do anything with it.'

She turned and looked at him, fresh tears brimming in her eyes.

'I just got lucky. It was as random as a narrow escape from a bullet. What if the sound of the sirens hadn't pierced through the forests? What if he hadn't left, knowing my screams wouldn't reach anyone?'

He extended his hand towards her, urging her silently back into his embrace. She went back into his arms willingly, wanting this closeness she had missed out on because of her misplaced guilt.

'All that matters is: you survived. You won that night and will also win back the rest of your life. You have to be proud of that.'

She sobbed into his arms a little more, coming to terms with the fact that she had wasted twelve years avoiding the healing process and the newness life had to offer.

'For so long, I thought it was my fault. That I crossed a line by turning up at your house with the indecent proposal, and I was punished for it.' She could feel his breathing change as he squeezed her a little tighter, very gently. When he spoke, his voice was heavy, courting a catch.

'I am sorry, Kavya. You will never know how sorry I have been for a long time for the part I played in all this.'

They stayed like that for a while, and Kavya felt calm and strangely sated. She released herself from his embrace and looked around the silhouettes of the unfeeling trees that stood there, witnessing this tender moment as emotionlessly as they had watched her getting mauled that night. It was as if the jungle had lost its power over her.

When they started back, Kavya saw Darsh removing his jacket and realised how uncomfortably warm she was too. The jungle trip had made them slightly sweaty, even on a cold night like this. She removed her pullover and tied it loosely around her waist, welcoming the cool breeze. Looking around, it suddenly came to her that up until that moment, she had followed the exact trajectory of that terrible night. She had jumped the wall and had sneaked into his house. She had met him in the living room and then walked out to the woods in the dead of night. It felt like she was rewriting her past, disassociating the places from the traumatic event.

Thirty-Four

On the way back, as Kavya sat behind him, she had no hesitation in slipping her hands around his waist. She leaned into him and snuggled closer. With the harrowing ordeal behind her, she could now appreciate the ride. It reminded her of the charged ride back from Jeeva Lake when they were teenagers. She had been on fire because of his proximity to her. She had daringly pressed her breasts into him and had closed all the gap between them, burning with want. Would she be able to feel that again if she tried? Wasn't she healing well? But she was not a teenager anymore. And she couldn't use him as a litmus test without his consent.

'What you just did, Kavya, in the forest, is actually what we sometimes legitimately use as part of therapy for trauma survivors. It's called exposure therapy. You expose yourself little by little to the things that trigger you. But it's key to have someone you trust or your doctor around.'

Kavya released an acquiescing grunt. That's what Dahlia told her when she recommended touching and holding people Kavya trusted. But she did not want to talk about it now. This experience had been overwhelming. For now, she wanted to think of happy things ... like this ride with him. As they turned into their lane and the shape of the towering white structure became visible, Kavya broke the silence by whispering her gratitude into his ear.

'Thank you, Darsh.'

She felt a subtle shift in his posture, a slight stiffening. She wondered if her words had unsettled him. Then he turned his head slightly, just enough for her to catch a glimpse of his profile. Before he could speak, she repeated, softer this time, 'Thank you.'

He looked back ahead, the muscle in his jaw tensing.

'Don't thank me,' he said, his voice rough. 'I have done nothing that deserves a thank you.'

He pulled the bike to a stop outside his gates. They climbed down and faced each other again.

'No, I mean it. Thank you. For Bangalore,' she said, her voice forlorn as it was time to leave.

Approaching him so that she was closer to him, she looked up into his eyes and spoke sincerely, 'You helped me take on this journey towards healing that I could never have otherwise.'

He opened his mouth to say something but closed it. Words were failing so Kavya went back into his arms, struggling with emotion.

Wrapped once more in the warm, protective circle of his arms, she turned deeper into the hug, turning her face into his chest. Her lips brushed against his bare skin, just at the hollow of his collarbone. The contact was barely a breath, but it lit a spark. A slight current ran through Kavya, reminding her of what it was like to feel physical attraction. Her lips lingered, just a moment longer than necessary. When she finally looked up, their eyes met. Kavya saw a flicker of what seemed like desire pass through his. She dropped her eyes, flustered.

Without a word, he reached out and slid two fingers under her chin. He tilted her face up, his thumb grazing the curve of her jaw, his eyes dark. Her breath caught in her throat.

She had to tell him.

'There's … something else that you should know,' she managed, her voice softer than she had intended.

'It's not just the darkness or the forests that scare me. Since that night, I … have had a compulsive fear of … touch … as in, anyone physically touching me, even if for a moment.'

She saw his eyes widen as he understood the implications of what she was telling him. He stepped back immediately, putting distance between them. His voice came out shocked, even a little terrified.

'I ... I am sorry ... I don't know why I did not notice...'

'No, that's the thing,' she interrupted him quietly.

'You … your touch … doesn't bother me. I don't really know why. Maybe because I know you from before the assault? But whatever, Darsh, the truth is … I hadn't been hugged for a decade before you turned up. And from the day you reminded me how warm physical closeness can feel, I have been craving it … quite a lot.'

He just stared at her in response. Kavya waited for pity but only saw a careful concern for her as he processed that information.

'Are things changing? After the last year of therapy?'

'I let Trisha hug me if that counts. It was not great, but I managed to not push her away,' she said, trying to sound casual, even glib. But the silence that followed from his side wasn't helping. Kavya looked away, suddenly aware of how much she had revealed and how exposed it made her feel.

He didn't speak for a long moment.

Then came his voice, low and unguarded. 'What about your desires? You've never ... wanted a relationship? Sex?'

Shame engulfed her. It felt like he had just exposed something broken inside her. And yet, strangely, she didn't want to hide anymore. There was something about the way he asked—not with judgement, but genuine concern—that made her want to answer.

'No, and I don't particularly mind,' she said quickly, meeting his eyes again. She tried to keep her voice even, to make it sound like the truth didn't sting.

But then, without planning to, the truth slipped out anyway.

'The only time I really wanted to sleep with someone ... was in this very house.' Her voice dropped. 'And it didn't end well.'

She turned her gaze back to the bungalow, her insides twisting with the weight of everything she'd just said. The silence that followed was thick, almost unbearable. She felt foolish, like a teenager confessing something raw and intimate, only to be met with awkward stillness.

She was about to turn, to retreat with what little pride she had left, when she felt his hand—gentle but firm—close around hers. He pulled her toward him.

'Do you still want to?' he asked, his voice barely above a whisper, but it landed on her skin like a touch and her breath stilled. She raised her eyes to his and found them focused on her with a new intensity. She knew she wanted to. She had agency now and she wanted to explore this newly awakened side of her. But why was he asking her? Was it because she had just told him he was the only one who could touch her? Because he saw it as a way to make up to her? Was it to assuage his guilt?

That wasn't what she wanted. Not like this. Not if it meant being a footnote to remorse. She shook her head, backing away.

"Don't do this Darsh," she said, quietly. "I know what you are doing. Don't."

Darsh's gaze didn't waver.

'Screw the past, Kavya. Screw that night. I am not trying to undo anything. This is now. I am asking you now. Do you still want to?'

She stared at him. There was a tightness in his jaw, a stillness in his frame, like he was holding himself back. Like if she said yes, he would break the space between them in a heartbeat.

It wasn't guilt. It was want. The realisation hit her like a live wire.

When she didn't answer , he stepped aside and pushed the gate open wider , giving her the choice to walk in if she wanted. She stepped through and he followed without a word.At the threshold of the house, he paused. The porch light cast a pale gold glow over his features, catching the sharp line of his cheekbone, the tension in his throat. It made his eyes look darker, deeper.

'You haven't answered,' he reminded her, his voice low, intimate.

She held his gaze. 'Yes,' she whispered finally. 'I want to.'

He stepped in closer, their breaths mingling now. His hand rose slowly, brushing through her hair to remove a dried leaf she hadn't noticed. But the gesture lingered, his fingers trailing down, gliding along the curve of her arm. Not hurried. Not hesitant. Just ... deliberate.

The touch was different. Nothing like before.

Kavya felt a slow stir inside her, a part of her long dormant beginning to burn.

His hand moved upward again, fingertips grazing the tender skin at the base of her neck, then resting lightly at the place where shoulder met spine. His thumb moved in a slow, circling caress. Her breath caught at the subtle, yet unbearably intimate contact.

She lifted her gaze to him, only to catch his eyes drop to her lips. Then, in a move so sudden and tender it sent a ripple through her, he raised his hand and ran his thumb slowly over her lower lip. Her breath hitched, and a soft unbidden gasp escaped, as something fluttered awake inside her. Her pullover, knotted loosely around her waist, slipped to the ground unnoticed.

He was watching her closely. Reading her reaction.

'I'm going to kiss you,' he murmured. His voice was velvet-soft. For the first time in years, Kavya felt desire. She was normal. Whole. And that simple truth made her heart expand.

Then she realised he was waiting, asking for her permission.

She nodded, almost shyly, and whispered a breath of a yes. Her eyes drifted shut as memory flickered—the one kiss they'd shared, the only kiss she'd ever known.

But the instant his lips touched hers, the past came crashing in.

A violent flash. A pain so sharp it stole her breath.

The memory of being bitten, bruised, punished for keeping her mouth shut, struck her with brutal force. Panic surged like fire through her veins. She tensed, teeth clenched, and pushed back with all the strength she had left in her.

To her surprise, there was no resistance. No one holding her down.

She stumbled back, chest heaving, and opened her eyes.

Darsh stood a few feet away, his expression stricken, his hands raised slightly, like he was afraid to move, afraid to speak.

Reality rushed in like cold air.

Her hands wouldn't stop shaking.

'I am sorry. I am so sorry.' Her voice quivered with regret.

'Don't say that,' he said, his voice dripping with barely contained anger, another emotion he had never shown before. He approached her again, but very slowly, only once she started calming down. Then he took her shaking hands and snaked his fingers between hers like always. There was an implacable expression in his eyes. He couldn't hide that he was battling his frustration inside.

'You don't need to be sorry. I have to be sorry. That asshole who did this to you has to be sorry, you understand that?'

Kavya stood there, stricken with hopelessness, feeling like a fool. Here was a man she desired, yet she couldn't bring herself to go forward with it. If this is how it turned out with him, there was no one on earth she could ever sleep with.

'I am damaged,' she said heavily, feeling lost as her eyes teared up.

'One step at a time,' he reminded her.

The trembling had stopped now that her hands were resting comfortably in the warmth of his hold.

'Let me drop you back, Kavya. To your house.'

'No,' she shook her head. 'I don't want to be alone tonight. Sleep next to me.'

Thirty-Five

Until one day ago, she could not have imagined sleeping in Darsh's room, but this night had been colossal in shaking the foundation of her notions. A slow but unshakeable conviction had burrowed itself into her heart. There was nowhere else she felt more at home than with him. The visit to the jungle had sealed his importance in her life. He had watched her fight and break and fight again, with minimal interference, yet his non-judgemental, rock-like presence had given her unimaginable strength.

A process of forgiving and acceptance that had begun the day she had stepped into Dahlia's office had culminated tonight, when she got rid of all her apprehensions, not just regarding him but also regarding her feelings for him. She loved him, but not in the fervent, obsessive way that made her a mess in her younger days. It was a love that made her feel grateful, like bright sunshine would make you feel when the clouds finally parted on a gloomy, dark day. Being around him now reminded her how she felt every morning when she spent time with her plants in the garden: at home.

She was terribly disappointed at how her body reacted to his attempt at kissing her, when every pore inside her wanted it. Everything had been so right about that moment, and she was ready to dissolve in his eyes, expecting more of the pleasantness her body had just begun to rediscover. But she had not anticipated the pain that came rushing in full throttle as she closed her eyes and felt his mouth on hers. Why did it have to be that way? Why, in her mind, was she able to welcome him, but her body refused to cooperate? In some ways, it was worse than before, when she did not feel anything at all.

She had fallen asleep the moment they went to bed, exhausted by the turn of events, but woke up in the thick of the night and, to her surprise, found herself alone. The musty odour, unique to the old bungalow, rushed to her nostrils, immediately reminding her where she was. A tall lamp in the far right corner of the room, with a cream lampshade, was left switched on, creating a play of shadows in the antique room.

The tiny coal fireplace that had fascinated her as a child now sat unused, old newspapers stuffed in the cavity meant for firewood. The archaic clock over the mantelpiece indicated it would be three in the morning. Not much had changed, except for the bed, which had been replaced with a larger one over the years. A loose wooden floorboard creaked as she lowered her feet, wondering where he could be at this hour. After checking the spare rooms, which seemed to have been locked for years and offered her a view of nothing but furniture covered in sheets with thick layers of dust, she climbed down the staircase.

He wasn't in the kitchen or the courtyard, so she turned towards the hallway to the living room and the balcony. She found him in the living room, sleeping on the sofa, just like last evening when she had first arrived. The room was warm and cosy from the fire. Clad only in a pair of grey joggers, he lay on his side, facing the door through which she had entered. Of course, she chided herself. He wouldn't be comfortable sleeping in the same bed as her, especially with her fear of touch.

Overcome with an unexpected urge to be close to him, she lowered herself onto the floor rug, sitting inches away from his sleeping face. He was beautiful, she sighed, wondering how wise it was to let herself fall in love like this again. The light from the reading lamp fell on his face like a pool of molten gold, highlighting the fine lines on otherwise smooth skin, which seemed to glow perpetually. His thick, upturned eyelashes shielded his mesmerising eyes.

It seemed like he had fallen asleep while reading again, as his arms were wrapped around a red leather-bound book, snuggled against his chest. Kavya's eyes glazed over the strong forearms that could have held her if she had not pushed him away. His fingers, now curled around the book, had brushed against her arms just hours earlier, sending her into a tizzy. She wanted him. There was no denying it. She let her eyes wander down to the toned muscles of his stomach, and then they hesitated at the drawstrings of his joggers. Scandalised by what she was doing, she turned her attention back to his face, only to find his eyes open, gazing at her silently.

Embarrassed, she fumbled for words.

'I'm sorry ... I just came looking for you because you weren't in bed...'

'And I see you found me a while ago,' he drawled sleepily, his voice laced with playfulness.

'Fine. I was admiring ... umm ... you ... a little bit.'

'See anything you like?' he asked, his tone teasing.

'Your eyes are always at the top of my list. It's like you have a different shade for every mood. I'm sure you hear it a lot.'

He raised his head slightly, propping himself up on his elbow, and studied her face with curiosity.

'Actually, no one's ever told me that before.'

'That can't be true. It's the first thing anyone would notice about you.'

He leaned back, resting his head on his hand as his gaze drifted over her face.

'What about you? Do you know the first thing people notice about you?'

Kavya averted her eyes, a slight flush creeping up her neck, not used to being looked at so intently.

'Don't do that,' he said, his voice gentle but firm. 'Look at me.'

She met his gaze again, and something shifted within her, an unexpected warmth blooming in the centre of her chest as he stared at her, like he could see her soul.

'Your entire face,' he continued, his voice quiet but steady. 'It's impossibly emotive. When you're angry, your eyes blaze. When you're happy, your face glows. When you're nervous, you bite your lip, and the colour rushes to them.'

His eyes rested on her mouth as he fell silent, and Kavya felt her lips go dry. Would he touch them again?

'You're doing it now, biting your lip,' he said, his voice low, his face hovering just inches above hers. So close. She wanted to touch him. No, she wanted to kiss him.

'Do it. I can see you're thinking about it,' he urged.

She almost raised her hand to touch his face but stopped, letting it fall back to her side as memories of the writhing pain from their last attempt to give in to their desire rushed back. That pain had incapacitated her, kept her frozen for minutes.

Sensing her hesitation, he leaned in closer, his voice now a whisper, each word heavy with certainty, filling her with a quiet strength.

'It's you who has the control. You decide what you want. You decide what you do. You decide when to stop or when to keep going. No one will ever take that control from you again.'

She gazed at his inviting mouth, and something within her shifted. She knew then; she had to.

'And don't close your eyes,' he added, a playful edge in his voice. 'Look into mine ... since you apparently love them so much.'

His face broke into a grin, the warmth in his expression reaching all the way up to his eyes.

Her heart stopped. She raised herself slightly and, in a swift motion, pressed her lips to his, eager to possess that smile, the one with the power to light up her very being. Even as she cautiously pushed her tongue into his welcoming mouth, she knew this time would be different. The simple act of initiating the kiss made her feel in control. *It's going to be OK*, she told herself, determined to stay in the present, refusing to close her eyes, even though every part of her wanted to.

He took his time responding, but when he did, his kiss deepened, his lips parting hers with a gradual intensity that sent tremors through her body. Yet, the dark imprint of the attacker's past touch still lingered on her lips, and she pulled back sharply, the sudden movement catching her breath. She was about to murmur another apology when he stopped her by gently placing a single finger over her lips.

When she fell silent, he slowly removed his hand. Kavya felt a sharp pang of loss at the absence of his touch. They stayed in the same position: Kavya kneeling on the floor, Darsh propped up on the sofa. She stared at him, feeling helpless, torn between the desire she could feel and the uncertainty of how to move forward.

This time, her gaze drifted over his body without restraint. That kiss had ignited something inside her, and for once, she didn't care if it showed.

'Do you know what you want, Kavya?' His voice was low, hoarse, betraying his own desire.

Kavya felt a blush rise to her cheeks, but she knew Darsh's question wasn't rhetorical. He was asking her to take control, to figure out the next step. She locked eyes with the carefully chiselled face she had spent years dreaming about, and in that moment, she knew exactly what she wanted.

'I'm going to explore you a little bit, Purohit.'

He nodded, even as the corners of his mouth turned up in a slight smile, seemingly both amused and touched by the innocence her words betrayed. Taking this as his consent, she climbed over him on the sofa. As she nestled comfortably, ignoring the sensation between her legs, Darsh folded his hands behind his head to show her he would not touch her. She would have all the time in the world to explore him without any hindrance from his side.

Kavya started by touching his face, going back to being the teenager who dreamt of this every day. Her touch was almost reverential as she explored it all: the forehead, the temple, the high cheekbones and the sharp jawline with a hint of stubble. Then she trailed her fingers down through the chest and the lower abdomen where she was sitting.

'You are so perfect,' she whispered, lost in her trip as she stroked the backs of her fingers back up through the packs on his stomach, through the sculpted chest to his face. When she met his gaze, she noticed his eyes had turned darker—the colour of sinful chocolate—but his hands stayed behind his head.

'We were sitting right here when you refused me, Darsh,' she said suddenly, the words slipping out before she could stop them. His expression shifted, guilt flashing across his features. Immediately, she regretted bringing it up, but she knew it was something she had to say.

'No, I don't mean to accuse you,' she added quickly, leaning closer and gently cupping his face, her eyes locking onto his. 'I want to apologise.'

Her voice softened with sincerity as she spoke, determined to take responsibility for her part. 'I'm sorry. For years, I made myself the victim and you the villain because I thought you rejected my love. But the truth is, Darsh, what I did to you wasn't OK.'

She took a shaky breath, her eyes searching his.

'That night, when I came into your house without your consent, and forced you into a situation you didn't want to be in … I objectified you. I am truly sorry, even more so because I can see you've been carrying that guilt with you. A guilt that isn't yours to bear.'

A single tear slipped from her eye and fell onto his upper lip. His gaze softened with tenderness, and Kavya felt the weight of his unspoken understanding. Without saying a word, he used his eyes to silently ask if he could reach for her, his hands still resting behind his head.

She nodded through the tears, offering a small smile. He gently tucked the stray strands of hair behind her ear, then carefully wiped the tear from her cheek.

'Listen to me,' he said, his voice low and steady. 'If you're not a victim, then neither am I. Somewhere inside, I knew I was hurting you, but I still kept showing up whenever I thought I needed you. I acknowledge that, and I accept it.'

'Uff, Purohit, you're even sexier when you talk about feelings,' she sighed dramatically, lifting herself up slightly, only for him to pull her back slowly, but with unwavering intent. Now, her body was pressed against his chest, and she could feel the warmth of his breath against her skin.

'I thought you were trying not to objectify me anymore?' His eyes bore into hers with mock annoyance, a teasing glint in his gaze.

She laughed softly, resting her head on his chest, feeling the comforting warmth of his presence.

'It's tough as hell. Have you met anyone who can get past your ... packaging?'

Darsh let out a deep laugh that vibrated through his body, shaking with genuine amusement.

'Packaging? Now I feel like an Amazon parcel. Thanks for that.'

She raised her head to drink in the sight of his laughing face. It was so rare to see him like that. She felt bolder and ran her fingers over his lips like he had done to her outside in the garden.

He stopped laughing, and the air became as charged as before her apology. Her nipples had perked up against his bare torso, with nothing but the thin fabric of her top and her bra between them. In response, she felt the backs of his fingers, which were in her hair, stroke from her temple down. Instinctively, she turned her face to meet them with her mouth, opening her lips a little.

His eyes were black slits as he pressed a knuckle gently to the edge of her mouth to check if she wanted it inside. Kavya sucked on them, egged on by a carnal need, and in no time, she was licking and biting his fingers, feeling increasingly empty.

She felt his other hand slip inside her top, and he placed a feather-like touch on her tummy. His eyes never left hers while his fingers explored her skin delicately, giving her time to process how she felt. She felt on fire at being touched like that, and it was evident Darsh could read it on her face because he grew bolder as he moved up, pulling the cups of her bra down to catch hold of her where she had never been held like that before.

She stilled, expecting fear and discomfort to overpower her again, and he sensed it. No words were spoken, but he kept her eyes locked with his, urging her silently but resolutely to stay with him, trust him, and let it all go.

Magically, she relaxed and could focus on the new sensations, which brought her a strange pleasure. As he tugged and teased her with his expert fingers, the pleasure grew and proved uncontainable. A moan escaped her lips as she adjusted to the bliss that shot through her.

In response to her reaction, his eyes darkened with blatant desire. She lowered her gaze to his lips, an unexplainable urge to kiss him rising within her. But she hesitated, fear tightening her chest.

As if aware of her thoughts, Darsh brought his lips closer to her ear and whispered suggestively,

'I could do a lot more with my mouth than kiss you, but you'll have to convince me you want it bad enough.'

Though it was barely a whisper, his voice was no longer gentle. It carried a bossy, mildly arrogant tone, laced with undeniable seduction. Shocked by the helpless yearning that threatened to consume her as the implications of his offer sank in, she jumped off him and moved away from the sofa.

He followed suit, his expression alert, a flicker of concern crossing his features.

'You OK?' His voice was softer now, but the intensity was still there. 'We can stop if you need to.'

She stared at him, her heart pounding in her chest as she marvelled at how exquisitely beautiful he was. His concern only made him more irresistible. She also noted how wet she felt between her legs after a decade, for the same man in the same room. At that moment, she knew she was ready. Her body had given her permission, causing her frozen feelings to melt into a warm, pulsating yearning that wouldn't be quenched easily.

She stepped forward and put her arms around his neck, speaking with an air of certainty.

'I want that ... what you just promised, and more. I want everything.'

His face relaxed, and he welcomed her into a close embrace. As Kavya leaned into him, her body unabashedly hungry for more, her touch turned more daring on its own accord. But even though he seemed to welcome her eagerness, she sensed he was holding himself back. There was a clear attempt to slow things down from his end, even though she had just confessed she wanted everything.

Seeing him exercising control, a sudden doubt assailed her because she couldn't stop the throbbing desire from growing stronger. She stepped back a little, looking at him inquisitively.

'You're not doing this just to fix me, right? Is this a charity?'

His jaw worked, and he inhaled sharply just before he pulled her back to him firmly. All the gentleness flew out of the window as he held her gaze with an intensity she had not seen before.

'Kavya, listen to me very carefully. I want you, and I wanted you that night. Almost as bad as I want you now.

'Do you think I ever forgot how beautiful you looked standing right here that night?

'In that black lacy lingerie, looking at me with your huge kohl-rimmed eyes, daring me to touch you? I was this close to losing it. You have no fucking idea how close I was to ripping all the lace off you.'

It was the first time he had mentioned that night. Strangely, the painful sting she felt when thinking about it disappeared. Knowing she had that effect on him made her feel bolder and wanted.

She took a few steps back slowly, away from him. Slipping both straps of her spaghetti top, she let it fall lower. Refusing to acknowledge the thumping in her heart and the urge to cover herself, she rasped, 'What about now?'

With satisfaction, she saw his eyes darken further in response. The desire in him was now as evident as hers.

'Darsh Purohit, I don't want to take it slow.'

These words came out of her like a command. He closed the gap between them in a second. The next moment, she was scooped up in his arms, and he was striding swiftly and urgently towards the stairway to his bedroom. It was evident he had reached the end of the restraint he was trying to practise with her.

Thirty-Six

Sunlight streamed through the slight gap in the curtains and fell right on Kavya's face, waking her up rather rudely. She stretched and turned on her side, reluctant to get up. Her eyes fell on the surroundings, and last night came rushing back to her. She turned around quickly, relieved to see he wasn't there. She wouldn't know how to be normal with him after last night.

Making sure she was alone, she smiled like a little girl, remembering how amazing it was. Not only had Darsh chased away all her fears of intimacy, but he had made her ask for it and beg for it, until there were no doubts left that she was completely ready, both physically and psychologically. When he had realised intuitively that she was nervous about him being on top, as it could bring back her claustrophobia, he showed her how great things could be in so many other ways.

He had been so patient with her, even as he broke through years of mental barriers, one after another, in showing her what her body wanted. And after the first time, when Kavya lost her inhibitions, revelling in the pleasure he introduced her to, she couldn't get enough of him. How did he feel about her? Inexperienced, unsophisticated, and selfish? He seemed happy indulging her demands, but he stopped abruptly when she whispered about loving him.

She sobered up as that part of the night surfaced in her memory. She was deep in the throes of passion, looking down at his perfect face when she said it aloud. *I never stopped loving you. I am so in love with you.*

The confession had caught him off guard. She could see his face harden, and soon after, he called it a night, giving her a small peck on the cheek. Oh, what had she done?

She planned to leave undetected, unprepared for the morning-after encounter, but he spotted her as she climbed down the stairway and invited her to join him in the kitchen. The open kitchen gave the entire house a pleasant aroma of ghee-rich cooking. She saw him flip a perfectly cooked thin dosa on the pan as he smiled at her, signalling for her to sit at the dining table. He displayed no signs of awkwardness, unlike what she was feeling, so she relaxed a little.

He served her the delicious-looking dosa on a plate and sat opposite her with a flask of warm water.

'Where's yours?' she asked, jabbing the thin crust with her hand, realising how hungry she was.

'I just finished a run. This, I made just for you,' he answered, bringing the flask to his mouth.

The chatter on the table fell silent as Kavya fixed her eyes on the dosa. Something inside her was stirring again, urging her to get up and cover his gorgeous mouth in a flurry of kisses, sit on his lap, or run her hands along the muscled packs of his stomach. Still, she restrained herself as the memory of his cold reaction before they slept jabbed the sides of her ribcage. It had started to hurt her the same way, and she wondered if it was foolhardy to have slept with him. She had wanted to use him as a bridge to cross over to a normal life, but the idea had fallen flat. She was foolish to think she could use him for anything without losing a grip on herself. Oh, what a mess she had made of things, she thought as her throat felt constricted again.

'Kavya, I wanted to talk to you.' She heard him from across the table and looked up. Trepidation knotted in her belly as a mixed dose of hope and fear ran through her.

'I am moving back to the US. I came here a few days ago only to close a deal for the house. I have sold everything that my family owned here.'

He had told her the same thing last night as well. She had been snuggled warm in the crook of his arm, feeling closer to him like never before, about to reveal her most important secret. And then he had broken the spell with his random announcement. He was doing it again just after they had shared a perfect night of intimacy.

For Kavya, it was slightly unsettling but still a welcome change that he was sharing more of himself with her, telling her his purpose of coming back and his future. So she decided to ask more.

'I remember you had plans to do something here for the Indian kids. You will have to travel back and forth a lot if you don't actually move here?'

No answer came forward immediately. He placed the flask on the table and shut down the lid slowly and deliberately, taking his time and swallowing more than water.

'All that has changed. I won't be coming back at all.'

Kavya felt something sink in her stomach. This was not just information-sharing from his part. It seemed like he was trying to tell her something else. Was he trying to tell her that she would never see him again?

With supreme effort, a carefully guarded expression, and a neutral tone, she masked her fears with another question that sounded quite casual.

'And when are you leaving for the US?'

He raised his hooded eyes to her hesitantly and answered.

'Tomorrow.'

Kavya stopped eating, caught off guard. There was something horrendously wrong with this situation. It did not sound logical, and Darsh never made illogical decisions.

'When did you book your flight?'

He didn't answer, but the expression of total resignation on his face as he tried to meet her eyes made it all clear. He was running away from her. He was abandoning her after last night because she had told him she loved him.

It perplexed her because she *knew* he cared. But could she be sure? This was Darsh. As a youth, he was fundamentally incapable of even basic empathy. Maybe he just masked his indifference better now. Maybe last night had been a charity, after all.

She had been feeling proud of her reflective behaviour after therapy, but now, faced with his confusing demeanour, her past trauma was raising its ugly head.

She pushed her plate away and leaned back in her chair to look at him squarely. Cold anger seethed inside her as she concluded that nothing had changed.

'So you decided this morning. Darsh, did you sleep with me out of guilt?'

He opened his mouth, but she cut him off. She didn't want to hear him.

'I thought you had changed into a different person, but one unfortunate utterance of the L-word and you're running away like a coward.'

'No, I'm not leaving because you said that. But honestly, Kavya, I had hoped you had grown out of it by now.' His voice came out quiet, but it cut through her like a knife.

'Fuck you, Darsh. You're right to decide to move back. Staying around you will bring me nothing but unnecessary complications.'

She stormed out of the kitchen, refusing to break down in front of him. She felt humiliated all over again once she realised the night had meant nothing to him. He didn't come after her. He didn't stop her.

Exactly like twelve years ago, she came back to her house feeling rejected. But this time, she would not crumble into pieces, longing for his love. She would go ahead and build a life that did not include him at all.

When Kavya descended the stairs back home, she immediately announced to her mother that she was flying back to Bangalore the next day. When her mother protested, Kavya pacified her by showing an interest in her matchmaking.

'Send me the profiles, Maa. Let's find me a good match; I'm ready.'

Later, she called Trisha to tell her she was returning to the office sooner than expected. Trisha was happy to hear that.

'Cannot wait. Wait till I tell everyone! You were missed, Kavya.'

'I missed work, too. I'm ready now.'

'Great news. Does that mean we can get back to pub-hopping? And meeting cute guys?'

'You bet. More so, as I'm not the frigid virgin you made fun of anymore.'

'Who did you do it with? Tell me you didn't sleep with a random stranger!'

'I slept with Darsh,' Kavya replied flatly. Just as she had expected, Trisha went quiet for a few seconds.

'Umm … what?'

'You heard me.'

'So … now … is he … are you…'

'He's the same loser he always was. He's running back to the US because he suspects I might get emotionally involved.'

'But you *are* already emotionally involved. I know that. He knows that.'

'Bullshit, Trisha.'

'He knows, Kavya. He wouldn't have slept with you casually. And he cares. He kept a tab on your health even after you kicked him out of your place.'

'Why are you advocating for him?'

Trisha sighed on the other end of the line. The memory of her last meeting with Darsh surfaced afresh.

He had sat there calmly, listening to her tell him how she felt about him. When she had started justifying herself, because she thought he wasn't taking her seriously because of her manner, he had stopped her midway.

'Why do you feel the need to justify who you are,' he had asked. 'You are who you are. Don't let anyone make you feel the need to explain yourself.'

'OK, but umm ... you're not exactly reacting to what I just told you ... about how I feel ... which is the point of this conversation,' she had said, as he avoided responding to her declaration.

He had remained silent.

'You think Kavya might not be OK with this because I asked her...'

'I can't see you. And it's not about you ... or even Kavya. I can't see anyone,' he had said, cutting her off, an edge in his voice. She had noticed then how stressed he looked, different from the times before.

'I need to know why.'

He had looked at her as if exasperated by her insistence. She hadn't imagined it. He was reeling from something personal.

'Tell me.'

And he had told her.

But it wasn't her secret to tell.

'I just happen to know some things you don't.'

'What is that supposed to mean?'

'Come back to work, Kavya. You're right. Forget him and move on.'

That phone call left her even more disturbed than before. What did she mean by saying she knew some things Kavya didn't? What was Darsh hiding from *her* but telling Trisha, someone he had known for only a few weeks?

She packed her stuff in stoic silence, having called a cab for five in the morning. All she had was one night left in this dreary town, where Purohit Mansion would soon be turned into a holiday home, cutting all ties with her childhood. It was a relief that her father was retiring in two years. It would leave her no reason to come back here and suffer the emptiness that Darsh would leave behind.

How cold did a person have to be to mechanically cut all ties with the house he had spent his growing years in? He had no dearth of money, but he was selling everything just to get rid of the town. Of her.

It was nothing to be surprised about, she thought wryly. He had always been unfeeling. The mask he had put on in Bangalore had been for a purpose. With the purpose over, he had gone back to being an ice statue.

But what was wrong with her? Knowing everything well, why was she falling for him again?

Frustrated, she paused from throwing her clothes into the suitcase and sat back on the bed with her head in her hands. *The night wouldn't leave her*. It had shown her how he could be under the bulletproof layer he had built around himself. He had made her feel like she was the only thing important to him, giving her a hundred per cent of himself, bringing her closer on a level that was much more than just physical.

She was in love with him. She had *always* been in love with him.

How had she ever thought she could walk away without fuss after sharing that level of intimacy with Darsh Purohit?

At dinner, she managed to convince her parents that it was a work emergency that had cut her trip short. After discussing their retirement plans, where she suggested they move to Bangalore with her, she returned to her room to spend her last night in Parvatnagar.

She glimpsed out the window for one last time with a heavy heart. The house was dark again, as if drawing the final curtains on the memories, discouraging her from peeking at it again. Turning off the lamp, she settled into sleep.

Thirty-Seven

Kavya woke up with a start as the window flew open with force, and a strong wind rushed inside. Her eyes followed a large mud ball that landed and rolled under her bed. Darsh was calling her in the same old fashion, as if they were teenagers.

She went to the window wearily and found him standing right beneath it, waiting for her. It was a cold and windy night, and standing under the bright full moon, he looked like a silvery ghost, holding his ground amid wildly swaying trees, against the loud swooshing sounds of the breeze all around. His jacket flapped hard against his body, revealing a thick shirt underneath, and his hair was wildly tousled. But he stood fixed to the spot like a rock.

'Come,' he said.

'No,' she shook her head.

'Come, or I'll climb up,' he insisted, dead serious.

'No, you will not,' she answered.

'I will. But it would be simpler if you came down.'

She reluctantly went down the steps after throwing on a jacket, reminding herself this was the last time. He waited until she approached him and then pointed to the bike.

'Come ride with me.'

She stared at the innocent-looking bike and remembered all the times she had gone with him on rides like this, even when her gut had told her not to. It was a moment of reckoning. This déjà vu allowed her to dissociate herself from her younger self, by breaking the pattern. Therefore, even though she knew she was breaking her heart, she shook her head firmly.

'No, I will not ride anywhere with you. In fact, I don't want to keep in touch with you at all after tonight. I'm very certain of that.'

He looked at her as if he expected her to continue explaining.

'Being around you, creating these nice memories, fucking hurts ... I don't want you in bits and pieces, here and there... I want you *forever*. And that's not possible. So why don't you just leave me alone?'

It took her every ounce of strength not to cry, but she didn't. In a deliberate effort to prove to herself that she had changed, she chose to be straightforward about her feelings—refusing to entangle herself in complications borne of unspoken words and false hopes.

He stepped closer to her, and under the gentle moonlight, she could see his features had softened. His face was almost wistful, as if he understood her anguish but didn't know what to do. His voice came out very gentle, almost pleading.

'Listen, Kavya, I don't want to repeat my past errors, and even though it's difficult for me to express my feelings, I *want* to make that effort. I don't want you leaving here thinking of me the same way.'

Kavya folded her arms across her chest, instantly defensive.

'So go ahead, I'm listening.'

'Not here. This place suffocates me. Come with me one final time,' he said, pointing towards the bike again.

He took her to Jeeva Lake, far from the suburbs and deserted at this hour. The ride was long, and the gusts of wind grew stronger with every kilometre. When they rounded the final bend, the lake appeared, shining like a flat metallic disc. Even as the wind ravaged the hilltops and trees, Jeeva Lake remained unruffled; its still surface kissed by the golden tint of the breaking dawn.

Darsh seemed lost in the view as they sat by the shore. Fireflies danced back and forth, weaving between the winds that swirled wildly through the nooks and crannies of the nearby rocks.

She turned to look at him. His profile was serious, meditative, and she was almost afraid to disturb the quiet he seemed lost in. Just when she thought he had forgotten why they were there, he spoke.

'What I'm going to tell you won't hurt you any less. But it will help you understand my reasons.'

He paused, and she braced herself for what was to come.

'I thought of you all these years—wanting to come back to see you—but I never had the courage. When Riya told me what had happened with you, it killed all my hope that you'd ever forgive me. And then I found out I was probably going to die.'

Kavya, shaken, thought she had misheard, but she stayed still, waiting for him to clarify.

'Just after I returned from dispersing my father's ashes, I was diagnosed with lung cancer. Turns out I inherited more than just my mother's unlovability.'

He exhaled slowly, his gaze distant.

'I never thought I'd mind dying, Kavya. But throughout the treatment, I kept thinking *if I had one more shot at life, I'd do so many things differently*. A lot of those things involved you. You kept appearing over and over again, and I realised I wanted to *live*.'

His voice broke slightly as he continued, but he didn't pause.

'After over half a year of tough treatment, the doctors told me I was cancer-free and had a real chance. So I focused on my health, like mad. I quit smoking, ran, followed a strict diet. I felt great. I thought I'd beaten it. So I came looking for you.'

His voice tightened, the words heavy as he let the truth slip out.

'But it was back. I found out in Bangalore the day you told me you wouldn't go out with me.'

He smirked bitterly as he finished the sentence, then turned to face her.

'Quite the irony, right? That day, I felt better than I had in years. I had asked you out, I'd enjoyed a long run in the woods... It was a shock, a reality check, to cough up blood again. My life was never going to be the same. I was forced to tell Trisha, as she was not taking no for an answer. Then I came back to your place, wanting to come clean but...'

She knew the rest. He had found her lying on her floor, naked and unconscious.

What did this mean? That when she was screaming at

him, bringing out all the filth she had stored in her guts ... when she had asked him to get out of her house ... he had been suffering from a relapse?

He had written her a letter owning up to things, analysing her feelings and asking her to get better ... all the while under the threat of his looming death.

She did not know what to feel anymore. It was as if she could see a blizzard of pain, guilt, loss and rage charging towards her, and she could do nothing but wait for it to hit her in full force.

His voice brought her back to the present.

'I went back again, and the relapse was caught early, so they could treat it with radiation. It looks like it's gone, for now. I'm lucky to have gotten my full health back after two rounds of treatment, but I don't know how long my luck will last. Doctors think it's very likely to return, given my family history.'

They both fell into silence. Kavya was frozen, unsure of what to say. The weight of everything he had told her hung between them like a storm cloud.

Darsh gently took her hand, covering it with his other, but this time, it didn't comfort her. It only made her feel colder. He spoke again, his voice quieter.

'Kavya, my life—whatever is left of it—will never be the same. Between strict regimens and constant check-ups, I wouldn't be much of a person to be with anyone. Yesterday, when you said you wanted to sleep with me, despite knowing I was leaving, I foolishly thought it was just about reclaiming control for you. But it's never just sex between us. I knew that even twelve years ago. How could I not know it yesterday? But I didn't have the heart to tell you.'

She saw the fear, the regret in his eyes, and it made him seem so ... human. The man who had always been the source of her longing and frustration, now vulnerable and exposed. She felt the tears welling up in her own eyes. Rage, unexpected and raw, swept over her.

'I don't understand you,' she choked out. 'Why are you making this about me? You're the one who is ... terminally sick!'

He stared at her, confused. Her tears blurred her vision, but she pressed on.

'Darsh, you can't just switch my feelings for you on and off. It's not yours to control. It's mine. The fact that you might die doesn't change how I feel. But what about you? What do you want?'

Silence fell again. This time, it wasn't uncomfortable. It was just ... heavy.

He looked down at his feet, swallowed hard, and when he spoke, his voice was tinged with exasperation, though he tried to keep it controlled.

'I've done nothing but ruin your life. And now that you're on your way to recovery, you can't possibly expect me to be OK with this. What will you gain from being with a man who will probably always be sick?'

'What's there to gain, Darsh? That's not how love works.'

He closed his eyes, pressing his palms to his forehead. She knew she was cornering him, asking him to face the truth about his cancer, about her, about them. He was fighting it, but she waited. After a few agonising minutes, he opened his eyes and met her gaze.

'So tell me. How does love work?'

She took a deep breath, trying to steady herself before asking the question that had been haunting her.

'Why didn't you tell me about it before we slept together?'

His answer came with a tinge of guilt. 'You know why I didn't. You had such an intense experience in the forest. I couldn't bear to break you with this news again. If I had my way, you would have never known.'

'Yet you did tell me.'

'Because you were breaking anyway. I saw you walk away this morning, and I felt that ... dejection...'

'You *felt* it,' she murmured. 'You felt what I felt.'

'Yes.'

'Maybe that's how love works.'

The silence after her words was deafening. It felt like the world had stopped moving. Even the fireflies' gentle humming seemed too loud. Darsh broke eye contact, resting his head on his knees and wrapping his arms around himself.

Minutes passed. Kavya looked away, her gaze caught by the horizon. The sun had crept up, spilling crimson light across the water, and the birds had started chirping softly in the morning sky.

'Darsh,' she said softly, her voice barely above a whisper. 'Look at me. Please.'

He raised his head reluctantly, but this time, his eyes were fixed on the rising sun. He didn't look at her.

'Do you want to do this alone? Or with me? I have a

flight to catch today, which means it's goodbye. Unless you tell me what you want.'

He turned to face her, his eyes reflecting deep sadness, defeat.

'I can't be so selfish.'

'But if you *could* be?'

'Then I wouldn't let you go.'

'Then don't.'

She inched closer to him, taking his hand, intertwining their fingers as he had done so many times before when she needed him. She felt him relax and lean a little into her.

'You realise this ... packaging, as you put it, would go, right? And life won't be all orgasms and fun.'

'Really? That's what you think this is all about?'

'There's nothing in here to love, Kavya.'

'And what makes you the authority on that?'

He tensed, a muscle in his jaw twitching before he cupped her face in his hands, his lips mere inches from hers.

'I'm scared. I thought I wouldn't mind dying, but you sticking around ... it changes everything.'

At that moment, Kavya felt the last distance between them fall away. He had let her in. She leaned in and kissed him on the lips. His eyes met hers questioningly, and she nodded. She was willing to go past her trigger with him.

He bent his mouth to hers, gave her a short kiss, and gradually went deeper. Faced with no resistance or distress, he finally let himself go. She felt the turmoil in his aggression as his tongue roved in her mouth without restraint. She lost herself in him, wanting to forget the life-shattering facts that faced them.

When he finally pulled back, their eyes locked. A single tear rolled down his cheek.

'Your eyes…' Kavya whispered, almost mesmerised. 'I never thought I'd see you cry.'

'You never thought you'd see me in love either,' he replied, his voice thick with emotion. 'But I love you. I think I've always loved you.'

She burrowed her head in his arms. She forgot the disastrous news he had just revealed for a moment, relishing the words she never thought she would hear. His arms tightened around her in assurance. It was as if he could read her thoughts. And everything felt just right, even if for a moment.

Acknowledgements

I wish to express my deepest gratitude to everyone who supported me throughout the creation of this book.

First, I thank my parents, Usha and Nagina Kumar Dubey, for instilling in me a love of reading from an early age—a passion that has been the cornerstone of my literary journey.

I am incredibly grateful to my beta readers for their thoughtful and constructive feedback. A special thank-you goes to Sreejeeta Ghosh, who proved to be a godsend by reading every version of this manuscript and offering brilliant ideas for improvement. I also extend my heartfelt thanks to my childhood friend, Deepti Agrawal, for reading the very first version and encouraging me at every step, helping me believe in this story and in my creative abilities. My sincere appreciation branches out to Simran Pavecha, whose ideas and insights, along with her excellent research recommendations, enriched this work immeasurably.

I would also like to acknowledge my other beta readers – my siblings and cousins: Shilpi, Shaswat, Siddhi, Kshipra, and Shruti – for their invaluable support and feedback. I want to also mention Akhila, Nimisha & Yashita for reading the very first draft and providing valuable feedback and encouragement.

A special shoutout goes to my son, Neil, who patiently waited for his bedtime stories while I worked through the chapters. His understanding and support have been a constant source of inspiration.

My heartfelt gratitude goes to my literary agent, Suhail Mathur and The Book Bakers, for the guidance and unwavering support in bringing this book to fruition. I am deeply grateful to author Neil D'Silva for connecting us at a time when I had almost given up hope on finding a good agent.

In closing, I must especially thank Om Books International for entrusting me with the chance to bring this story into the world. Their impeccable team made the journey an absolute pleasure.

